THE MOUNTAIN MAN'S BRAT

KITTY GRAHAM

Published by Blushing Books
An Imprint of
ABCD Graphics and Design, Inc.
A Virginia Corporation
977 Seminole Trail #233
Charlottesville, VA 22901

Kitty Graham
The Mountain Man's Brat

Print ISBN: 978-1-63954-156-0
v1

Chapter 1

Bree Phillips was delighted when she saw the glacier pond and lush meadow in the distance. The people, the music, the food, and the regular beer at the guest event set up by the mountain resort she was visiting were boring. She decided to trek to the top of a ridge opposite the activity to observe the scenery from a different perspective. The hike across the wide meadow to the base of the rocky ridge where she began climbing took longer than she anticipated. She was panting as she topped the rise and wished she'd brought along a water bottle. Bree turned back to evaluate her progress and congratulated herself for hiking so far on her own. From her new vantage point, the dually pickups, SUVs, and all-terrain vehicles looked like beetles and flies on the landscape. The people appeared as pinheads and the music was completely out of earshot.

The Dallas debutante stood on the ridge top and believed by standing there, she had proof of her ability to navigate the great outdoors and take care of herself. She wondered why people made such a big deal about the difficulties and dangers of spending time in the wilderness. Bree had her phone in her back pocket, so what could possibly go wrong? Upon catching her breath, she began threading her way down and through a boulder field that sloped in the opposite direction of the ridge-line where she had been standing. Bree worked her way around one rock, then another and another until she cleared the boulder field and was now well over an hour's climb away from the resort's staff and the festivities. It never occurred to her to notice or make a note of any landmarks she could use to find her way back to the group.

Topping the next rise, Bree was parched and feeling over-heated from her exertion even though she wore light athletic shoes, short shorts, tank top and a light cotton long sleeve shirt tied around her middle. Her stubbornness won out over her discomfort, and she continued to press on toward the top of another ridge. Bree wasn't going to be easily deterred from experiencing the adventure she was creating for herself. She was eager to see what lay before her and kept moving. She came to the top of another slope where she carefully stepped over a felled barbed wire fence and briefly wondered why someone would put sharp, rusty wire in the road for her to step on. She continued walking. Bree Phillips was so engrossed in her climb, she failed to notice the dark clouds gathering behind her.

Newton Meyers followed the tracks of the rabbit he was hunting and was easily closing the gap between him and his quarry. Newt loved his life and his solitude and believed people really had little to offer him other than aggravation. He both observed and despised their complete lack of awareness and how their actions often ended up destroying the very things they purported to love. As a former park ranger and game warden, Newt struggled not to seethe whenever he saw people just ruining everything. He cherished the land, all of it, and he especially loved the Rocky Mountains. The more Newt saw the land being torn up, the more he believed former park ranger and writer Edward Abbey had it right: Leave wild places the hell alone if you genuinely love them.

Colorado's recreational tourism campaign created even more overuse in what he called a 'come live here and destroy everything' campaign. Newt thought a backwoods literacy class should be mandatory before folks were ever allowed on the trails. People had to take hunter's safety classes to shoot a gun, and he was convinced that people easily did more damage by their brainless wanderings than they would have if they were shooting at actual things.

He continued tracking the rabbit for his dinner and was looking for a clue as to the animal's whereabouts. Newt gazed at the sun to get an idea of the time. It was past its zenith, so it had to be nearing three o'clock in the afternoon. He looked around and noticed the clouds were building overhead and were unusually dark, forecasting a gully washer. When rain dropped from the sky like that, the trails filled with water and could become treacherous. Newt wanted to be back to his cabin with dinner in tow by the time the rain cut loose. He knew the rabbit would be looking for a place to rest while the storm moved in, and Newt wanted to do the same. He hoped to find the animal soon, and as he approached a small copse of Aspens, his quarry burst forth from the underbrush. Newt quickly dispatched the animal with his .22 and walked over to the crumpled form. He congratulated himself on the clean kill and the fine dinner he'd enjoy once the rabbit was dressed and roasted.

Bending over to pick up his prey, he noticed the gray color of the storm clouds had deepened to a greenish black. Newt could see lightning flickering within them and decided not to hang around to see how much rain was waiting to drop. He turned in the direction of his small homestead and kicked his gait into a trot before the rain began to fall in pelting drops. The first wet blotches bounced off his body, and Newt crossed the threshold into his modest space and set the rabbit near the backdoor. He always left his doors open when the storms came through since he loved listening to the rain even though he hated being in it. Newt turned to walk back into the main room of the cabin when a brilliant flash of light showed every detail in the space. The illumination was followed immediately by a crack and boom loud enough to make his teeth rattle.

"Well, my friend, we made it just in time," Newt said to the rabbit as he walked back to stand by the door where he watched the sheets of rain score the ground and the winds shake the evergreen trees.

Bree became aware of the change in the light when she found it was more difficult to follow the delightful forest trail she had discovered. When Bree first entered the woods, she found the forest enchanting and imagined that fairies and gnomes lived among the rocks and bushes. Bree could see herself as Snow White waiting for her prince to find her, rescue her, and love her forever. Deep down inside, Bree entertained the fantasy of being a princess. She wanted a strong and handsome man who chose to spend lots of time with her. Bree played out fantasies about how he would dote on her and provide for her every wish and keep her safe from the threats and troubles in the world.

Bree lacked nothing in the material realm. Her father always gave her whatever she wanted as far as material things were concerned. He also handed her lots of things she didn't want, especially because she felt nothing he ever gave was without his attaching a considerable obligation. And stuff wasn't what Bree wanted anyway. She wanted to have a loving connection to her father, but his business ventures were his mistresses and demanded all of his time. His lack of attention toward her always left Bree feeling empty and alone.

She knew she wanted something more for herself but hadn't yet decided exactly what "something more" entailed. All Bree knew was the life she was currently living wasn't it. She continued to walk through the enchanted glen, caught up in her daydream and began to wonder if maybe the mountains held the key to what she wanted. After all, here she was 'roughing it' and the freedom she experienced as her new adventure unfolded was a heady experience.

Bree continued walking deeper into the trees when a frigid wind suddenly kicked up as the sun slid behind the dark clouds. She untied her cotton shirt and quickly pulled it over her arms and shoulders, but the gusts cut right through it. She'd no sooner gotten the shirt over her bare skin when a blinding flash of light, followed immediately by a deafening boom, caused her to scream. She had no idea what to do next. Were trees safe in a thunderstorm? Should she get out into the open? Should she find rocks to hide behind? Bree panicked. She didn't know how to be safe. Before she could decide what to do next, the rain fell all at once, just like it had been poured out of a bucket in the sky. She ran toward the cover of the trees, but as she sprinted across the uneven terrain, her foot hooked into a tree root, and she fell flat, not even having a chance to catch herself. The rain continued to drop in sheets as the trail flooded and water ran over her twisted ankle, soaking her shoes. The deluge drenched the rest of her. She fumbled for her smartphone and pulled it from her back pocket, only to find she had no signal. Bree was desperate now and did what any urban princess in distress would do: she sat up and screamed as loudly as she possibly could, hoping someone would come to her rescue.

Newt was enjoying Nature's show as he watched the rain wash the forest. He was glad to see the late summer moisture since it was sure to inhibit the wildfire danger which was an endless worry to him and a constant threat to his property. He served as a volunteer firefighter and was glad the rain might save him some long days of working a front line.

He listened to the rain fall and let the chill of the wind blow over him. The pounding downpour hit the side of the cabin, but in the distance, he thought he heard another rabbit screaming close by. The eerie sound, like a child screeching, indicated the animal was in trouble. Newt looked down at the rabbit he'd dispatched earlier and decided that having two for dinner would be better than having just one. He was a big guy, and he was famished. If he could get an extra entrée for an easy catch, it might be worth getting a little wet for. Stripping off his shirt and slipping on an old pair of muck boots he used for chores on his property, Newt grabbed his .22 and headed toward the noise emanating from the trees.

He came through the wooded area and found the trail becoming a river as water coursed over it. The screaming continued. Newt's vision followed the sound, but he didn't find an injured rabbit; instead, he found the very last thing he wanted. A drenched and frightened woman was sitting in the gushing stream that had been a trail just moments ago. She was dressed scantily, and the few clothes she had on were pasted to her body. The sky kept lighting up and the thunderclaps were right on the lightning's heels. Each time it flashed, she screamed. Clearly, she was terrified, and Newt was moved to help her. Without thinking a moment longer, Newt started running in his battered muck boots on the uneven surface. It was no easy feat for him to continue lumbering toward her. When Bree saw the strange form staggering in her direction, she screamed even louder. The thing looked like a Neanderthal.

"I'm not going to hurt you," Newt shouted.

Bree shouted back to him. "Help! I'm hurt! Oh, please don't harm me!" she cried as the stranger came closer.

Newt reached down and carefully lay a comforting hand on her shoulder as he appraised the situation. "It's okay. I'm here to assist, so don't worry. I need to know what's hurt before I try to move you." He could see she was a bit scraped up, and her ankle was starting to swell, but her injuries didn't look life threatening.

Another flash followed by a crash of thunder sounded. She shrieked again as her panic took over. Her responses became hysterical.

"Breathe and tell me what hurts," Newt said, gently trying to coax the answer from her as the rain poured around them.

Bree finally caught her breath and articulated an answer in between her sobs. "I fell. I hurt my ankle."

"Don't worry. I've got you now and I'm here to help you. Come on, I'll get you back to my cabin where you'll be safe and can dry off, and I can tend to your wounds." Newt bent down and picked up the mud-covered woman, turned, and walked in long strides back toward his cabin. The poor thing was terrified and chilled to the bone, and Newt wanted to protect her. Pulling her closer to him to share his body warmth, he briefly wondered if the isolation was getting to him. Why would he want to shield a stranger, especially when he didn't want people around to begin with? He pushed those thoughts aside and carried her to his cabin. The thing to do now was put first things first.

Bree was stunned at how the man just reached down and picked her up like she was a stuffed toy. He was so big and so powerful! She closed her eyes and leaned her head into his chest, marveling at the comfort she felt from the warmth of his body. He held her close and carried her away from the muddy trail, and she didn't have a care in the world just then. He smelled like pine and musk. She looked up to see the face of her champion. His sable hair was tied into a man bun and scruff along his angular face reminded her of a disheveled GQ model. His eyes were so dark they looked like they were made of obsidian. Bree unexpectedly found his wild earthiness appealing; he was exotic and interesting. The man carried her out of the trees, and she saw a cabin that looked not much bigger than a shipping container. Bree hoped that was where he was heading since it had to be dry and warm. She couldn't wait to be inside since the rain was intensifying if that was even possible. The wind was still howling, and the man pulled her in more closely before he vaulted over three steps that led to the screen door at the back of the house. He pulled the door open with one of the hands supporting her and soon brought her into a little kitchen space where he settled her onto a chair.

"Stay here," he told her.

Bree nodded. She was shivering uncontrollably with the cold and the wet trapped in her clothes. She watched him walk across the room and down a little hallway to an area that must have been his bedroom. He returned with a heavy Pendleton blanket and brought it over to her.

"Stand up so I can put this around you," he said in a no-nonsense manner as he approached her.

"Okay," Bree said trying to control her chattering teeth. She couldn't remember ever having been so cold! And she couldn't recall feeling so compelled to respond immediately to someone's demands.

"You just sit there and warm up while I get some water heated. I'll make you some nettle tea, and then you can tell me all about what happened. I'm Newt, by the way."

"Bree." She nodded and pulled the blanket closer while he set a blue, porcelain-coated metal coffee pot atop a burner on the small stove.

"I don't think you have more than a sprain. I imagine this tea I'm making will take the edge off unless you are in tremendous pain. If you need more relief, I can give you some willow bark." He turned to regard her and surprised to be taken by her beautiful deep brown doe-like eyes. She was a filthy, soaked mudball, but she was looking at him with those long lashes and a pitiful expression, and his heart did a little flip in his chest. She was an adorable little train wreck!

"Thank you for helping me. It's a good thing you came along when you did. My stupid phone didn't have any signal," Bree managed to blurt out now that her teeth were no longer rattling her jaw.

"Yeah, you don't usually get signals up here. I like that about living here and being off the grid."

"Why?"

"I don't like people being able to find me unless it's on my terms."

"Why?"

"You ask a lot of questions."

"And you don't answer them, so what?" Bree snipped. She didn't like how he was so direct and assuming. "How did you find me anyway?"

"I was anticipating I'd find a wounded animal and not a wounded woman. I thought you were an injured rabbit and was coming to get you for my supper."

"Oh!" Bree looked stricken. "You mean you were going to kill a bunny and eat it?"

Newt noticed her horrified expression. "Don't eat rabbit, huh?"

"Eww! I'm vegan. But I do like to have bacon with my pancakes."

Newt held her eyes with a stern expression and said, "Bacon is cured pig."

"Yuck! What do you mean by 'cured'?"

"I mean they soak it in salt and sugar or maple syrup after the hog is butchered."

"Are you some kind of barbarian?"

"You just said you're vegan but eat bacon," Newt stated as he carried steaming tea in a metal camping cup over to her.

"I know what I said," Bree lifted her chin, daring him to challenge her.

Newt lifted his eyebrow in response to her attitude. "Any-way, here's your tea." He set the cup on the table in front of her and then moved to stand against the wall since his other chair was outside on the porch.

Bree tasted it and screwed up her face into a grimace. "It's bitter!" she complained.

"Yeah, it probably is. I think I still have some honey." Newt walked over to a cupboard and returned with a pint canning jar filled with honeycomb. He grabbed a metal spoon from a drawer and stuck it in with the honey before setting it in front of her.

"What's that?" This time she curled her lip.

Newt again noted her response and could clearly see she was spoiled. "It's honeycomb," he patiently explained. "Dip the spoon along the edges to get the honey, and don't beat up the wax while you're doing it. I use the comb for other things like candles once the honey is gone."

"You're a strange person." Bree gave him a look like he'd just grown horns.

"And you're just like most of the other clueless people I've met," he said, except he knew that wasn't quite true. "So, what are you doing up here and why are you so poorly prepared for the conditions?"

"Well, I was at a cookout and decided to go for a hike," she answered breezily.

Newt gave her a stern look. His voice sounded flinty. "Without a jacket, sturdy shoes, a hat, trail map, whistle, or even a water bottle?"

"I guess I didn't know I needed all of *that*." Bree looked down at her hands which she had folded in her lap. She felt embarrassed.

"A cookout you say?"

"Yes, I'm staying at the Mount Goliath Resort. The staffers drove us up to a meadow where we played games and had a cookout. The people were boring, so I decided to take in the sights instead."

"The resort. If you were involved with the activities, I am sure the staff members are missing you by now. I'll bet they started looking for you and had to pull everyone back because of the storm. Did anyone see you leave?"

"No. Why?"

"They don't have any way to know which direction you went and where to look for you. Don't you know you need to tell people where you're headed in case you can't get back?"

"Oh, they said something about that, but I thought I could manage." She waved her hand dismissively.

"Clearly, you did just fine. That's why you're here with a strange man in a strange cabin." Newt's statement dripped with sarcasm. "Where are you from?"

"Dallas."

"Texas? Nothing in the Rockies is anything like Texas! You're lucky I heard you and that you aren't hurt any worse than you are. Where's your accent?"

"I don't really have a strong one, and it usually only comes out when I'm around other people from home."

A strong wind gust buffeted the side of the cabin and rain pelted against the windows with renewed force. Bree looked around wide-eyed.

"Well, Bree from Dallas, I need to get you back to the resort. I'm sure they'll send out a search party in the morning since it's too dangerous for them to look for you tonight. It's also too dangerous for me to escort you back right now. I'll guide you to where you belong in the morning."

"Why can't we go back now? Don't you have a car?" she asked, her voice twinged with annoyance.

"No. Even if I did, I just said it's too dangerous to go out tonight. The streams will be swollen and possibly impassable. You don't just go out in weather like this without being able to determine what hazards might be present."

"So, you're saying I have to stay here until morning?" Bree said in a higher pitch than she intended.

"That's exactly what I'm saying."

"Oh, are you now?" Bree tipped her chin toward the ceiling and crossed her arms in front of her.

"I am."

Bree's eyes narrowed. "I want to go home now!"

"And I just told you that it's not safe to go back tonight. You are lucky you aren't my girl. I'd have you over my knee, warming up your sweet behind right about now. Consider yourself lucky. Since you're a guest, I won't."

"You wouldn't dare do that to someone."

"I would if I cared about her, and she acted like you just did. I'd have her beet-red bare bottom facing me while she stood in the corner and reconsidered her behavior."

"You can't treat women like that!"

"I don't tolerate childish attitudes. Act like a brat with me, missy, and you get disciplined."

"You really are a barbarian."

"No. I would be demonstrating a measure of my care and concern." Newt exhaled deeply. "I am not going to spank you. I will, however, fix you some dinner and give you my bed for the night so you can sleep comfortably. Go down the hall to the bathroom and wash up for supper. I'll get you set up for a proper shower after we eat."

Bree stood up, watching him with a wary expression. Newt steadily met her gaze and watched her turn slowly and start walking down the short hallway. The hem of the blanket was dragging across the floor, and she looked like a little girl as she moved out of sight.

Dinner was nothing fancy, but Bree was famished and didn't care when he placed a simple scrambled egg sandwich and some canned peaches in front of her. Newt excused himself to bring in the other chair from the front porch and go dress out the rabbit he'd planned to have for his own supper. He wanted to get them into his small fridge, so when he returned home tomorrow, it'd be ready for roasting.

Bree ravenously downed the sandwich and then began scooping the sweet peaches into her hungry maw. She'd never had something so simple and yet so delicious. Newt returned to the kitchen and was amused when he saw Bree's empty plate and her sheepish expression.

"I guess I was hungry," she said as she looked up at him. "That was really yummy. Thank you."

"I'm going to make a sandwich for myself. Would you like me to fix another one for you?"

"Oh, yes, please!" Bree happily bounced on her chair.

Newt smiled, swished her plate off the table and got to work. Shortly he brought back full plates and set them on the table. He was delighted to see Bree's eyes light up before she resumed eating with gusto.

The conversation ebbed as they finished their meal. Once both plates were empty, Newt stood up, looked at Bree and said, "I promised you a chance to clean up, so let me get you started with a shower. You can sleep in one of my shirts and a pair of my drawstring pants if that's okay, you'll swim in them, and it's not the high fashion you're probably used to. I'll give you some wool socks to keep your feet warm. The clothes are clean, cozy and dry, and good enough to sleep in."

Bree smiled as she thought about washing off the day's adventure and willingly followed him to the tiny bedroom where he pulled clothes from a dresser and handed them to her. Then he gave her a folded beach towel and washcloth. A large tooth comb sat on top of the stack he gave her. Newt led her to the bathroom and leaned into the tiny shower stall to begin running the water to warm it. He pointed out what bath products he had available for her to use. "You'll have to make this a quick as possible. I store most of my water. Once the tank is used up, I have to bring in more or purify it myself. You have ten minutes, so don't goof around in there or else you'll have shampoo in your hair until I get you back to the resort. I consider wasting water a serious offense."

Bree could see from his stern expression that he meant business, and once he pulled the door closed behind him, she quickly shed her muddy clothes and got underneath the water. The pressure and the temperature weren't as high as she was used to, but she was glad to see the dirty water flowing down the drain. She was dried off, dressed, and combing her hair when Newt knocked on the door indicating that time was up. When she came out of the steamy room, he handed her a new toothbrush. Bree noticed he, too, was freshly washed.

"How did you get so wet?" she asked.

"I washed up outside while you took your shower in here."

"Wasn't it cold?"

"Of course it was, but why use stored water when Mother Nature is providing what I need? That rain is still falling steadily." Newt moved past her and started toward the kitchen. He picked up the heavy blanket he'd wrapped her in earlier. "I put some water to boil on the stove. We can have one of my herbal tea blends before we turn in. A bit catmint tea should do nicely."

Bree cast him a doubtful look.

"Trust me," he said as he approached her with the blanket and wrapped it around her. "It tastes fine, and it will relax you. Go sit down on the loveseat, and I will bring it to you." He gave her a reassuring nod.

Not long after Bree got comfortable, Newt showed up carrying two camping cups and the honey jar in a shallow baking pan he used as a tray which he set on the roughhewn coffee table. The loveseat faced a stone fireplace, and Newt began stacking kindling on the grate before he added a couple of split logs and lit the paper at the bottom of the pile. Once he was certain the flames were strong, he joined Bree and handed her one of the steaming cups.

Bree hesitantly tasted the hot tea and found it satisfactory, even without honey.

"Want it sweeter?" he asked. "I'll add some honey for you."

Bree nodded, and he dipped up the golden honey and stirred it into her cup.

"So, now that you are dry, warm, fed, clean and safe, tell me why you left the resort."

"You can't imagine how boring it was. I couldn't stand it any longer and decided to make my own adventure."

"Which, as I told you, was a foolish thing to do. Didn't anyone ever teach you how to be safe in the mountains?"

"Well, you know I'm from Dallas, so I never really had occasion to learn. I just didn't think about it."

"Are you staying at the resort alone?"

"Yes."

"Why?"

"My father sent me up here for my college graduation and to get rid of me. He owns that resort and several others, so it wasn't like he took time to plan anything for me. His employees put everything together, but it was still lame."

"I'm getting the sense that you and your father don't have the best relationship."

"Well, after my mom died, he married his mistress, which is his work. I think he was relieved when Mom was gone because he didn't have to divide his attention any longer. He left me with the household staff to figure things out for myself. That is until he needed to brand his empire and entertain clients; then, he wants me around since my image is on most of the advertising for his company. He says I'm the face of Exclusive Retreats." Bree's voice took on a sardonic edge.

"Are you?"

"Yes, but not by choice. He could have hired someone else to do it, but this way he can control me and make me be his corporate poster child or make me host his stupid parties. Mind you, he only has anything to do with me when he needs me to do something for his business."

Newt's voice was soft and sympathetic when he asked, "How long ago did your mom die."

"I was eight. Like I said, he left me with the house staff. I had a nanny for the first year, but since I didn't get into any trouble, my father started leaving me with the housekeepers and grounds' crew. They were always nice to me. I think they may have felt a little bit sorry for me because he was gone for long stretches. I spent most holidays with the staff." Bree's lower lip was trembling as she looked down at her hands.

"But it still sounds like you had everything you needed, especially if the staff was good to you."

Bree lowered her head so he couldn't see her eyes cloud over. "Yes, I had everything I could ever want—except his attention. That's what I really wanted. I still hope for it even though I am grown up now." She choked back her tears, and once she was sure she wasn't going to cry, she looked up at Newt. "So, what's your story? Why do you hang out here in the middle of nowhere all by yourself?" She took a sip of her tea and looked at him expectantly and then had to look away. His direct gaze pinned her to where she was sitting, and her body flushed with unexpected heat. Now that she was safe and comfortable, she couldn't help but notice how handsome and commanding he was.

"I told you earlier, I'm out here in the middle of nowhere because I like it."

"Don't you have a job or something?"

"I used to work for the Colorado Division of Wildlife as a Game Warden, but any job in law enforcement wears on a person after a while. I busted up a big poaching ring and helped send a few guys to jail for a long while. At first, I was hoping to promote. Instead, I decided to move to a new area before they get done with their sentences, which is coming up before too long. I decided I didn't want to be around to meet them again. My uncle, on my mother's side, made it possible for me to relocate as he left me a nice and unexpected financial gift. It affords me the freedom to do whatever I want to keep a modest revenue stream going to pay taxes on the property and buy new equipment for making my custom furniture. It also funds the improvements here. My needs are met, and I am happy taking care of myself."

"Do you know how to build furniture because you're from around here?"

"No. I learned to build furniture on my own when I

was younger. It started out as a hobby and has become a side business. I started specializing with the beetle-kill pine after my friend Owen, who is a native of the area, talked me into moving up her. Owen worked with me to get the poaching ring busted, so we've known each other a while. When I ended up with the money from my uncle, Owen suggested I buy some property here. I like the area and thought it would be nice to know at least one person if I went to a new place. I took him up on his offer five years ago. When I first got the property, there was nothing but old ranch buildings to work with. I've been slowly restoring the original structures and making improvements to the place. So far, I am happy with what I've done and look forward to getting my next batch of projects completed."

Bree pretended to be interested in his plans, but there was something else that popped into her mind when he began talking. She shifted her position to face him directly and looked into his eyes. "But don't you get lonely? I mean, I have the staff at home, and I still feel empty because my father isn't there like I want him to be."

Newt heard the kind concern in her voice. "I rarely find people I like well enough to have around for more than an occasional meal or maybe a couple of beers."

Bree squirmed as she tried to build up the nerve to ask him what she really wanted to know. "I just met you, but I can't help but be curious about something you said earlier."

Newt lifted an eyebrow as he invited her to share. "Yes?"

"You weren't serious about that spanking thing, were you?"

"Of course, I was. You can bet I am determined that any girl I am serious about will behave herself. I believe a genuine and lasting relationship needs not only lots of nurturing, but also clear boundaries. If those boundaries, which I lay down for her safety and well-being, are not obeyed, then it is my responsibility to discipline her."

"So, you *are* a barbarian."

"Look, a disciplinary spanking demonstrates my measure of care and concern for her. If she deserves it, I will spank the woman I love because I cherish her. The swats I administer to her sweet bottom and the resulting sting serves to remind her how much I care."

Bree's brow furrowed with confusion. Newt reached over and covered her tiny hands with his large, strong ones. His voice softened when he said, "If I spank, it's because I care."

"I guess I would have never looked at it that way. I've only been threatened with a licking and was always terrified of it." Bree shifted uncomfortably. His idea of genuine concern and clear governance titillated her, and she hoped he couldn't see her blushing in the firelight.

Newt sensed the change in her demeanor and was beguiled. She was so damn adorable, and it was everything he could do not to pull her into his lap and kiss her. He tried to divert his thinking and noticed the rain was beginning to lighten up. "Hear that? The rain is moving out, so I'll be able to take you back to the resort in the morning. But right now, my girl, you need to get some rest. Tomorrow, we have a long hike back." Newt stood up, offered her his hand, and lifted her to her feet. "I insist you take my bed tonight."

Bree looked at him with her wide and beautiful eyes. "But I want to stay up and talk some more. I'm not tired yet."

"Yes, you are. You've had a big day and need your rest. I'm certain you don't even know how tired you are. Right now, you need someone to make sure you are taken care of."

Bree pouted as he led her down the short hallway and into his bedroom. He pulled the covers down and patted the bed. "Come on. I'll tuck you in."

"Tuck me in? Like a little girl?"

"Yes and wish you sweet dreams until morning." His voice was calm and reassuring.

Bree crawled into the bed and lay down. Newt pulled the covers up to her chin and then tucked the blankets snugly around her form before looking down at her and brushing a stray tendril of hair from her face. "Sweet dreams," he said before he left the room and pulled the door closed behind him.

Bree wanted to call him back, but the steady drumming of the rain on the roof and the comforting weight of the blankets lulled her into closing her eyes. She was soon breathing softly and fast asleep.

Chapter 2

Newt stood quietly outside the bedroom door until he was confident Bree had drifted off into an exhausted slumber before he retrieved her muddy clothes from the bathroom floor, and carried them to the kitchen. He filled the teakettle with water and stepped outside the back door to retrieve the wash tub which was hanging outside. The rain was slowly and intermittently splashing now, and he could see patches of starlit sky as the storm clouds had moved off to the east.

He brought the washtub into the kitchen, poured the hot water into it and tossed in a handful of soap shavings before he added Bree's muddy clothes to the mix. He carefully scrubbed the items clean and took them outside to rinse in captured rainwater. Once he was satisfied everything was spotless, he set up a drying rack by the fireplace and draped the wet items over the rungs. He leaned down to stir the coals beneath the grate and added more kindling and wood. With the fire stoked, he knew the thin cloth would be dry by morning. With his chore completed, Newt settled back onto the loveseat and let his mind wander as he watched the flames lick at and ignite the wood.

He reflected on how much had happened since he dispatched that first rabbit. Not only did he have two rabbits prepared for roasting tomorrow, but he also had a beautiful bratty woman sleeping in his bed. He was intrigued by more than her attractiveness. Clearly, she needed someone to care for her, and Newt struggled with an internal conflict. He loved his solitude, but he never expected to meet someone like sweet Bree from Dallas. Sighing, he stretched out on the loveseat, his legs draping over the far arm while his head rested on the other. The position was by no means comfortable. No matter, he didn't anticipate he would get much sleep anyway. Newt closed his eyes and listened to the crackle and pop of the fire and recalled her large, expressive brown eyes and impish smile. It wasn't long before he, too, was breathing evenly and fast asleep.

Gray light filtered through the blue checkered café curtain covering the small window in the cozy bedroom. Bree stared at the wall and the light, trying to piece together where she was. Her sleepy cobwebs parted, and she realized she was comfortable and safe in Newt's bed. She stretched luxuriously and lay still, waiting for the rush of blood to clear her head. The dim light indicated it was entirely too early to be up and around. She rolled over and tried to go back to sleep, but the smell of food wafted on the air, and Bree's stomach growled loudly. She groaned, but her empty tummy wouldn't cease its demands. She sat up and placed her warm, wool-clad feet on the floor and started walking toward the sound of pots clunking together and the smell of fresh coffee. She'd no sooner come around the corner when Newt looked up and smiled broadly.

"Good morning, sunshine! You're just in time. I was just getting ready to come get you for breakfast." Newt reached over to the coffeepot that sat on the stove. He poured her a steaming cup and handed it to her. "Do you take anything in your coffee?"

Bree reached toward the cup, gratefully. "No. Black and bitchy is exactly how I like it." She inhaled the earthy scent of the dark liquid.

"Me too, but we'll just say 'black' from now on. I don't abide cussing from ladies. How'd you sleep?"

"Uhm, okay." Bree looked into the dark liquid as she chose her next words. "I slept well. You were right, I was more tired than I realized. I feel amazing now."

"Yeah, the mountain air does that to you. It also makes you really hungry, so I fixed us a filling and energy-packed breakfast for our journey to get you back to the resort. Go wash up and come sit down. Breakfast is almost ready."

Bree nodded and started walking to the bathroom. She thought she heard a tinge of melancholy when he mentioned taking her back, but she didn't know him well enough to be sure and suspected she might be hearing what she wanted to hear. The thought of going back to the resort and leaving this unusual and handsome man made her feel wistful as well.

When she returned, she found the kitchen table was set with two steaming bowls of oatmeal topped with dried fruit and nuts on top. Canned milk sat on the table next to the honey jar, and it was clear he had just topped off the coffee. Newt walked over to her when she approached the chair she'd sat in the night before and pulled it out so she could be seated. After helping her move up to the table's edge, he walked to the opposite side and took a seat himself. "As you can see, we have steel-cut oats, dried berries, and hazelnuts. I opened a can of milk in case you'd like some over your oats." He picked up the can and prepared to pour some into her bowl.

"Yes."

"Yes, what?" he demanded as he looked right at her.

"Uhm, yes, please?"

"That's better. I know people from Texas are taught good manners. Say 'when'."

"When," Bree said. "Thank you," she added before he could scold her again.

"That's better." Newt scooped up some of the hot cereal and placed it in his mouth, and Bree watched his strong jawline as he munched his breakfast.

She took a spoonful and was delighted when the flavor of the dressed-up oats tickled her tongue. "Gosh, this is really good!"

"It pleases you, then?" Newt's eyes shone with delight.

"Yes."

"Perfect."

They finished the meal in a quiet and comfortable silence. Both were famished, and there wasn't anything else that needed to be said at that moment. Once their bowls were polished clean, Newt stood up and looked directly at Bree. "Now, you stay right there and let me bring you some more coffee. I have something I'd like to discuss with you." He stacked the dishes and walked over to the sink where he eased them into the sudsy water and returned with the coffeepot.

Bree smiled and stayed put until he returned and handed her cup to her.

Newt pulled his chair to the corner of the table so he could be closer to her and reached over to take her hand. She didn't flinch and he took that as a good sign. "I told you last night that I am not very fond of other people. I have to tell you I enjoyed hearing about you and explaining to you the type of relationship I would be interested in. All that being said, I feel like there is some kind of connection, you know, something between us and wondered if you were feeling the same way."

Bree's face flushed with heat, the color creeping into her cheeks. "You're an interesting person," she said with an airy whisper.

"Interesting like a cool rock or a pinecone, or interesting like you want to know me better?"

"Like I might want to know you better."

"Okay, I am going to escort you back to the resort today. I want to give you time to think about whether you'd want to be in a nurturing, yet disciplined relationship. I will wholeheartedly welcome you if you decide being adored and cared for works for you. I want you to think seriously about this because you must be in a relationship with me of your own volition. Promise to consider what I said?"

Bree was stunned and could only nod her head to say yes. She felt giddy knowing he wanted her to come back, and that feeling skipped from her belly to her hips and further down. She resisted the urge to squirm on her chair in case he took it to mean she was uncomfortable with his suggestion.

Newt reached over and tipped her chin up to him. He gave her a light kiss, like faerie wings. "We're going to get you back to the resort now, so go change your clothes. I washed them for you last night, and you will find everything laid out on the bed."

"You washed my clothes?"

"I did. I told you I'll take care of you."

The trek back to the resort was anything but peaceful. Bree's complaints were endless. Newt wondered how it was possible for her to find so many things that were wrong as he led her back along the trail on which she had managed to get herself lost. He was concerned about her comfort since she had wrenched her ankle when she hooked her foot in the tree root the day before and kept assuring her that if she would just keep moving, she would be able to walk off most of the pain. When she groused too loudly, he would stop to put his arm around her to help her walk and picked her up to carry her over the particularly rugged terrain. They followed the trail back over the ridge Bree had initially crested earlier when she ended up on his side of the mountain. Before too much longer, they stepped over the downed barbed wire fence and began walking down the slope toward the huge meadow.

"You know that barbed wire represents a border, don't you?" he asked as they walked past it.

"Really? There wasn't a sign or anything."

"It's vast up here, and a homesteader can't have signs every five feet on their borders. It's not as if most folks would even pay attention to a sign if they saw one. Actually, I think notices are usually interpreted as invitations to trespass."

From the ridge they could see a few resort vehicles at the site where Bree left on her adventure the day before. There was also a small group of people, which Newt assumed were part of the search and rescue team, along with a few resort staff members. Newt and Bree were nearly across the meadow when someone in the group noticed them and called out to the others. Everyone began running toward them, and when the group caught up, Newt could see the relief now flooding the faces of those in the rescue party. Clearly, they were concerned for Bree's safety. An auburn-haired staffer whose nametag read "Jessica" escorted Bree over to a truck with the resort logo and wrapped Bree in a silver emergency blanket. Jessica handed Bree a bottle of water.

One of the male staffers approached Newt, handing him a bottle of water too.

"No thanks, I brought my own," Newt said as he waved away the one-use plastic bottle and showed his hydration pack.

The man looked over his shoulder and leaned over to speak to Newt. "God, I can't tell you how glad we are to see her. We caution the guests about wandering off, and they usually listen. This is the first time we've had one go missing for more than a day. I can't tell you how worried we were. She's the owner's daughter, you know. Thanks, man."

"Sure thing," Newt answered before he walked over to the pickup to find Bree sitting in the passenger seat. "I'm going back home now. Think about what I said." He smiled warmly and pulled her close to him in a powerful embrace.

Bree struggled not to melt into his arms. "I promise I will. Thank you for rescuing me," she said and hugged him back.

Newt turned and started hiking back toward his home. Bree watched him go as Jessica began asking Bree lots of questions about where she'd gone and how she was feeling, which Bree answered without thought. She kept watching Newt as he climbed the first ridge. He didn't look back before he disappeared over the other side. She felt a stab of sadness but didn't let it linger because now she wondered if Newt the mountain man hadn't seen the last of her.

Bree was back to her room shortly after she said goodbye to Newt and the resort staff returned her to the lodge safely. She excused herself from Jessica's care and returned to the room she'd had before her departure. Everything was just as she'd left it, although her time in the room seemed like years ago. Bree realized she hadn't once thought to check her phone when she was with Newt because she learned it did no good. Now, she was connected to the world once again, and she groaned outwardly when she noticed that she had voicemails.

Four were from her father. There was no surprise there. He probably had some function he wanted her to cut her trip short for, so she could do his bidding. There was also a message from a number that wasn't familiar. Bree did a reverse lookup on it and found the call originated from a law firm in Fort Worth.

Bree knew the message from her father was a tirade about his not being able to reach her, so she called the number for the law firm first.

The phone rang twice before a cheerful voice answered. "Dickens and Dickens Law Firm, this is Jenny. How may I help you?"

"Uhm, hello, Jenny. This is Bree Phillips. I received a message from this number. A Mr. Robert C. Dickens left a message asking me to call him back."

"Thank you for calling back Ms. Phillips. I'll connect you."

The phone rang only once and was answered by a soft-spoken male's voice. "Good afternoon. How may I be of assistance?"

"Bree Phillips. You left a message for me."

"Ah, yes, Ms. Phillips. It is so good to finally reach you. Nearly ten years ago, your mother came to see me and asked that I set up a trust for you based on her family's assets. It's a considerable sum, my girl. Your mother specifically asked that you not become privy to the trust until you completed your college education. Also, she was adamant that your father know nothing about it."

"Excuse me. What are you saying? That I my mother provided an inheritance for me?"

"Yes. A considerable one. She didn't let your father know about her wealth because she feared he would take control of it for his business ventures rather than make sure it provided for your wellbeing."

Bree's head was spinning. "Are you telling me that I am independently wealthy now?"

"I am. Your mother wanted you to be free to have a life that you would love and to make sure you would never, ever be second to a man's ambition. I shall send the documents to you for e-signatures. Let me know where you'd like the disbursement to go, and we are all done."

"Mr. Dickens, I really don't know what to say. Thank you. Thank you so much!"

"Not at all. Your mother was a special woman, and it's tragic that she left us so soon. I do believe she would be extremely proud of your accomplishments, so promise me you will continue to live a happy life and reach for the stars."

Bree struggled to control both her tears and her elation. "I will. Thank you so much!" Her hands were shaking when she ended the call, and true to the attorney's word, the documents soon arrived in her email. Bree signed them with a new sense of hope for her future.

Her next call wasn't going to be as uplifting, and she dreaded having to speak to her father. The phone rang and rang, and Bree hoped her message would go to voicemail, but he picked up at the very last moment.

A terse and hurried voice sounded on the other end. "Phillips here."

"Hi, Dad," Bree said flatly, bracing for his tirade.

"Where the hell are you? I've been trying to get ahold of you for over twenty-four hours!"

"I went for a hike yesterday and got lost. Then a big storm came up, but someone found me and brought me back to the resort today."

"I should have asked them to watch you more closely. No matter, you're going to cut your trip short and come home. I have an important client arriving for dinner the day after tomorrow. You need to be here to host."

Bree struggled to keep herself from yelling at him and chose her words carefully. "Father, I'm not cutting my trip short; in fact, I am not even sure what I am going to do when my stay here is over." She took a deep breath and continued, "I can tell you I am going to take a few more weeks, maybe even months before I come home."

"Who is going to host the party? Breanna, you are being unreasonable."

"I am not being unreasonable, Father. Ever since Mom died, you have acted like I am a doll you can pull down from your shelf whenever you care to be entertained or want a decoration. I'm a person, Father, and I have things I want to do besides being the face of your company."

"You will come home tomorrow, Breanna. You have a duty. I pay your way. If you don't, there will be serious consequences."

"Such as?"

"I'll… I'll cut you off. You can't possibly support yourself. You don't even have a job. You'd better think long and hard about what you are saying to me, Daughter."

"Father, I love you, but I can't do this right now. So much has changed, and I have to decide what I want for myself. Don't bother calling me back. My mind is made up. I will let you know when I decide I am coming home."

"You're being silly. What earth-shaking changes could you possibly be talking about? Breanna, you are going to regret this."

"I love you, Father. Goodbye." She pressed the button on her phone to end the call, blocked the number, and threw the phone onto the bed before she let her head fall into her hands and let her tears spill over.

Bree sobbed for what seemed like the entire afternoon but eventually felt the heaviness lift. She climbed off the bed and shuffled into the posh bath area to briefly contemplate taking a soak in the deep tub. She realized she wanted to remember the time she'd spent with Newt the night before and took a hot shower instead. Bree stood underneath the warm water as it streamed over her hair and body. She let her mind wander to Newt's admonishment the night before about wasting water and quickly soaped up and rinsed off. She pretended he was waiting outside the door to chastise her for taking too long.

After dressing in her pj's, she combed the tangles from her hair and then lay out on the bed with her arms folded behind her head, trying to recall the discussions she'd had with the unusual, handsome mountain man. She was free to go find him now, but she wasn't sure, at least intellectually, that she wanted to be in the type of relationship Newt had described. Bree rolled over onto her belly, wondering what it would be like to have her rear reddened. She couldn't help but squirm when she thought about his stern expression and his strong hands disciplining and then comforting her.

Chapter 3

Newt topped the rise and trekked back home. He couldn't keep his mind from pondering the beautiful Bree and how he'd reluctantly enjoyed the diversion of rescuing her. He also knew that if he saw her again, he'd have some serious lessons to teach her about the dangers of the mountains. She was obviously headstrong and thought she knew what was best for her. Little did she know she had much to learn, and he was the man to teach the spoiled woman with a few solid swats to her sweet bottom. He smiled as he envisioned her lying over his knee, her rear bared and ready for him to smack. If she were to stay in the high country with him, she'd have to be taught how to keep herself safe in the wilderness by listening to him. If she returned, Newt was sure he'd be redirecting her behavior on a regular basis.

He pulled his thoughts away from her and reflected on how he enjoyed his simple life of hard work and few distractions. Newt especially appreciated how little social contact he had and liked his own company. He rarely found another presence he could tolerate for more than an afternoon. Still, no matter how he tried to focus on his love of a hermit's existence, his thoughts kept going back to the beautiful, vulnerable woman. Sure, he thought she was silly, yet he saw something else beneath her girly veneer and suspected there was another side of this woman she didn't have time to reveal him. His intellect shouted at him that she'd only get in his way and keep him from achieving his goals, and for a little while, Newt listened to his rational voice. But his heart simply didn't want to resign itself to not getting to know the beautiful wide-eyed girl better.

The next day, Newt was carefully sanding a section of Lodgepole for a custom furniture project. The tree had been killed by Mountain Pine beetles and had an unusual character. He was creating a solid niche market for his craftsmanship in working the infested wood and was also investing into biochar technology, so it could become mainstream. He paused his work to look at his cabin and around the cattle shed he'd restored. Both the improvements he'd made on his property and his woodworking skill made Newt want to puff up with pride. He'd been making upgrades for the past fifteen years and that progress came from staying focused on his goals and bringing them to fruition.

The cattle shed he used as a shop provided the room he needed to create his revenue stream, and he could also field dress the animals he hunted for food. He had a dry place to store his tools and keep his projects away from the elements and marauding insects, although, sometimes he didn't mind just covering the mired bodies over with the thick varnish to create an even more artistic piece. Newt loved convincing the squeamish urban clients that seeing bugs on the kitchen table is hip, not disgusting and enjoyed persuading them it was a modern version of amber. Newt thought the hipsters and the industrial tourists were the silliest, most ridiculous people he'd ever run across and found the outsiders insufferable.

Bree slept poorly, her mind reminiscing the previous night with her rescuer. Her body burned with the curiosity and desire to feel his touch. She began to consider what Newt said regarding the type of relationship he would insist upon, and now she intended to act upon what he told her. Bree slipped on a t-shirt, lounge pants and sandals and made her way to the front desk. If she was going to follow through on her plan, she needed to get more information.

The auburn-haired woman who assisted Bree upon her return to the resort was sorting invoices at the front desk. The morning was new, and the guests demands few as most were still snoozing, so the woman could concentrate on her paperwork.

"Hi, Jessica. Jessica. That's right, isn't it?" Bree said as she approached the desk.

"Good remembering," Jessica said with deliberate cheerfulness and internal dread. The last thing she wanted to deal with this morning was the owner's daughter.

"Do you know Newt? The man who rescued me?"

"I know of him. He has a homestead over the ridge. I've only seen him a couple of times when I go over to the next canyon to pick up last-minute necessities for people. Guests forget things all the time. This is a resort, so sometimes they aren't particularly patient and can't wait until I go to the big box stores in the town on the highway.

"The next canyon over you say?"

"Yes, there's a small mountain town over there with a quaint café and a mercantile. They sell things like over-priced groceries, postcards, fishing licenses and supplies, ammunition, trail maps. The sort of things people need before they start hiking into the woods."

"How long does it take to get to the town?" Bree's voice was bright and tinged with excitement. "I love café food. Do you know if they have croissants and salads? A light brunch would be delightful. Maybe a mimosa or two would be just the thing to set the tone for an adventure."

"It's not café food like that," Jessica replied, struggling to hide her annoyance. "It's more the greasy spoon variety. If you like biscuits and gravy or fried eggs and steak, you won't be disappointed. I think the salads over there are iceberg lettuce with drained, canned vegetables over the top, and of course, an enormous side of ranch dressing."

"Yuck! You're not messing with me, are you?" Bree's eyes narrowed with suspicion.

"Of course not. What reason would I have to do that? You asked me a question. I'm just being honest."

"Sorry. I guess it seems odd that there are no fresh alternatives. We have lots of unique bistros at home in Dallas. There are so many options: smoothie shops, some Indian and Thai restaurants, sushi joints and one really yummy vegetarian market that has the most amazing entrées and gluten-free baked goods."

"Well, you're in a different part of the country now. These areas were originally settled by folks as wild and free as the areas they tamed. The urban trends are part of the workings for resort areas, but they take a long time to reach native populations, if they ever do."

"Do you know a lot about the people around here."

"I grew up in the canyon I was just telling you about, so yes, I'm familiar with folks in the permanent population."

"Do you like working over here?"

Bree didn't notice the resentful edge tinging Jessica's reply. "There's not a lot of work outside of tourism in these parts, and hospitality is where the jobs are." Jessica looked down to hide her frustration. Arranging a fresh smile on her face, she looked up and continued, "And I get to meet so many nice people, like you," Jessica looked at Bree and forced herself to flash a dazzling smile this time.

Bree excused herself and walked back down the hall to her lavish room. She opened the blinds once the door was closed behind her and watched the sunlit trees. She felt drawn to them and longed to be among them. Her father had arranged for her to stay three more nights at the resort. Today, the staff would be taking guests down the canyon and divide the tourists into groups, so they could enjoy a whitewater rafting trip. The day after that, the visitors would have an option of fly fishing or horseback riding. None of the activities appealed to Bree. She wasn't much of a water fan, so the rafting trip, while adventurous, wasn't her idea of fun. Were the resort taking them to a roller coaster, she'd go for that. Fly fishing was completely out of the question. What would she do if she caught a fish? She certainly wouldn't eat it! And she could ride horses any time at home since her best friend showed Arabians in western pleasure and equitation events all over the country.

Bree had another adventure in mind: to find Newt the mountain man. And she knew what she had to do next. Walking back into the hall, she retraced her steps to the front desk. Jessica was now folding gold cloth napkins into fans for the morning brunch and was carefully placing them into a clear bus tub.

"Hi again," Bree said as she approached the desk.

Jessica quietly sighed. "Hello again," she said looking up from her folding.

Bree placed her elbow on the edge of the desk and leaned over to talk to Jessica in a conspiratorial manner. "I'm checking out early and leaving today." Bree winked, turned, and walked away before Jessica could try to dissuade her.

Once Bree was back to her room she took a shower and prepared for her departure. She felt giddy with excitement and practically gulped the Greek yogurt, fruit cup, and gluten-free toast she'd had room service deliver while she started packing. Bree filled her suitcases with the clothing she wasn't going to need on the trail such as her most current fashion items, bikini, and impractical shoes. She'd stow everything in the trunk of her rental car while she was on the trail. Bree set aside items she planned to take with her: skinny jeans, a few t-shirts and tank tops to start. She packed two button-down shirts and, of course, her yoga pants and several changes of underclothes.

It occurred to her she probably needed to look the moun-taineer part, so she headed down to the resort giftshop and selected items she thought she might need. Bree purchased a mid-sized, sturdy backpack and got some advice from the store clerk about which over-priced hiking boots to buy. She selected a coat with a liner that could be unzipped from the outer shell. The layers, the clerk told her, were supposed to keep her warm when the temperature reached zero degrees. Bree didn't believe for a minute that the temperatures got that low in the summer and thought the clerk was messing with her. She let it go. She was eager to get moving and didn't want to deal with calling someone out for thinking she could be so gullible.

The clerk continued to make recommendations, so she bought a collapsible felted wool hat with a stampede string, an alpaca scarf, and woolen mittens even though she was positive she wasn't going to need any of the outerwear. Finally, she picked out a large water bottle and a spray can of SPF fifty sunscreen. At the last moment, the clerk brought a tube of citronella mosquito repellent and a stick of beeswax lip balm. Bree added them to the tall stack of items near the register when she noticed a display with fancy pocketknives while she was waiting to check out. One knife with a bone-colored handle had a carved image of a horned rabbit which caught her attention. Bree had never seen anything like it and wondered about the horns on a little bunny. She figured it must be an animal particular to the area and decided she wanted to know more about it. She could ask Newt when she took it to her rescuer as a thank you. Maybe that kind of rabbit was the kind he was hunting when he found her in danger. Bree pointed out the knife she wanted and asked the clerk to add it to her stack of purchases. She paid with the Black American Express card her father provided for her and took the items back to her room to get everything packed together for her departure.

Chapter 4

Once her BMW M3 rental was loaded up, Bree hit the road. She didn't have any problem following the directions Jessica had given her for the drive to the next canyon over and arrived at the tiny mountain town shortly after noon. The word 'town' was a loose definition of what Bree discovered. It was a wide spot in the road, from what she could tell, and nothing close to the definition of a town in the Dallas area. This unfamiliar territory just added to Bree's sense of adventure as she parked her car at the end of the empty, flat dirt area in front of what she could only guess was the local grocery store. Underneath a large sign that read *Moose Mercantile* sat a building that looked like a long log cabin with a wooden walkway stretching the entire length of the storefront. Bundled firewood and ten-pound sacks of charcoal were stacked up next to a small, bagged ice freezer near the front door. An old, wooden screen door painted a glossy red served as the main entrance. Bree pushed the surprisingly heavy door open, and a friendly bell chimed the happy announcement of a customer.

A handsome, kind-looking older man looked up from his

conversation with, who Bree assumed was, another local. Both men wore cargo pants, t-shirts, and lightweight hiking boots with wool socks peeking over the boot tops. The proprietor wore a red shopkeeper's apron. They were seated at one of the small tables drinking coffee and playing dominoes.

"Looks like you've got a live one here," said the local. He sported wild brown hair and an untamed beard. A brimmed hat hung down his back from a stampede cord. The man had on a well-worn and faded light gray shirt with the slogan *Bigfoot Rides Mountain Bikes.* Bree was amused by the depiction on the shirt. The Sasquatch on the bike didn't look too far removed from the tall man wearing it. She also noticed the large gun he wore in a holster at his side and thought it odd that a wild man would be open carrying just like many of the clean-cut residents of Dallas.

"Something I can help you find?" asked the man wearing the apron. Bree guessed he was the owner of the store as he was better groomed and seemed to care that she'd come into the store.

"I don't think so. I just need a minute to look around," Bree said as she tried to figure out how she would get the information she was looking for. She let her gaze move over the establishment and saw several small tables lined the perimeter of one half of the store. A dilapidated loveseat with an equally forlorn coffee table in front of it created a nook. Old board games and magazines were stacked so high on the table that a person would have to move something to set a cup of coffee on it. A food counter with an ice cream case sat below a menu board. To the right was a small cabinet with a pump coffee pot, a large container of powdered creamer and granulated sugar, some metal spoons and mix-matched mugs. The sign posted by the coffee invited patrons to fill a cup and leave a donation.

The opposite side of the store had a few lines of shelves

with a limited grocery selection, over-priced and rarely in demand personal care items, camping supplies, and tourist trinkets. At the end of one aisle was a rack of postcards and a sign posted on the top advertised postage was available at the register. Another rack was half filled with cheap sunglasses. Next to the counter that supported the register were two small refrigerators. One sported a sign advertising 'Worms'. The other fridge contained a surprisingly wide selection of soda and only one brand of bottled water. There was a larger cooler behind the checkout counter chilling sixpacks of local craft beer. Next to the beer cooler was a narrow shelf with shot bottles and pints of hard stuff.

"Bet she needs worms," Bigfoot said with a wicked grin, clearly suggesting that worms would be the last thing a prissy tourist would want.

"Knock it off, Owen. Miss, I'm Emmett Olsen. Owen here has bad manners. Since I own the joint, I get to boss him around."

"Whatever," muttered Owen as he stood up with his cup and shuffled over to the coffeepot.

"Actually, I need help finding someone. Do you guys know where I can find a guy named Newt?" Bree grabbed a diet soda and moved toward the register.

The big man turned around and gave her a look of disbelief. "Newt? Really?. You want to talk to Newt? You know he doesn't like people, right?" The scruffy man was incredulous.

"I do, but he rescued me, and I want to give him a present to thank him for his help."

"Don't mind him," the older man said. "Owen just happens to be heading in Newt's direction. Isn't that right?" Emmett leveled a direct look at Owen. "I think you should escort her so she can thank her champion. It's not every day someone does something sweet like returning a kindness." The proprietor's voice had a demanding edge.

41

"Uhm, sure. I suppose I need to take that big furniture order to him anyway since he comes into town so infrequently," Owen grumbled. Lifting his mug and tossing back the last of his coffee, Owen deposited his cup into the bus tub by the coffeepot. "We can finish our game tomorrow. Don't move the pieces. I know you cheat."

"If I cheat, then your coffee is free tomorrow," Emmett said as he handed Bree her change, and she slipped the soda into her backpack.

"It's always free," Owen carped.

"Mister, is it okay if I leave my car here while I'm gone?" Bree asked the store owner.

"I don't know. That parking lot's pretty full," Emmett teased her. "Of course, dear. Leave it a few days if you like. It'll be safe here. No one except me will even know it's here since there's hardly any traffic this time of year."

"Thank you. I really appreciate your help." Bree was checking the zippers on her pack when she saw the large, rumpled man start heading toward the door without any announcement. Bree quickly slung the pack strap over her shoulder and jogged to catch up before she was able to fall into step behind him and followed him to a rusty, faded blue and white 1978 Ford four by four. Bree had serious doubts the truck would even start.

"Get in," Owen gruffly demanded.

Bree ran around to the passenger side, reached up to open the door and threw her pack on the floorboard. The vehicle sat high, and Bree struggled to pull herself into the cab. Once she was seated on the cracked, black upholstery, Owen turned the key and the old truck roared to life. Without a muffler, the truck sounded like an angry cougar as it climbed the steep, poorly defined mountain road. Bree looked over at the driver who initiated no conversation whatsoever, and she wondered if everyone in the mountains was socially inept. The abruptness of these men she kept bumping into was vastly different from the Texan gentility she was accustomed to. Bree couldn't decide if she found it intriguing or off-putting.

The truck continued its ascent for what seemed an eternity since the only sound came from the booming engine as it worked up the slope and approached a flat area. Owen snuggled the truck's passenger side right next to a rock wall, jumped out, and began to trudge away in the direction of what looked like a thin ribbon of a trail. Bree realized he was leaving without her, and quickly grabbed her pack, vaulted through the driver's door and out of the high cab. When her feet hit the ground, she began jogging to, once again, catch up and puzzled over why all the guys around this area seemed to have giraffe legs.

There was no time to enjoy the hike. Bree was racing to keep up with her guide and forced herself to kick it into high gear. The further she went into the woods, the more eager she was to see Newt and hoped he would be happy to see her. Bree wanted Newt to smile when he saw her gift, but more than that, she wished to show herself as a capable person. Bree smirked at her cleverness and scurried after the tall man. Owen began scaling the side of a steep rise before he disappeared. It took her several strides until she could reestablish a visual on him and anxiously wondered if he was still on the trail before she caught sight of him again. She also questioned whether the thin ribbon of dirt they were following could even be called a trail. Bree scrambled up the rise, fell, scraped her knee and groaned in frustration. She just knew Newt was going to think she was accident prone. Bree ignored the sting and clamored up the ridge. Now, Owen was completely out of sight. Fortunately, there was only one way Bree could go on the trail, and she continued to doggedly follow it.

Newt was so absorbed in his work that he didn't see his friend Owen cresting the rise to the east of the property, quickly stalking toward the old lean-to.

"Hey, you better get ready. You got a visitor," Owen said abruptly, making Newt drop the sanding block he was using.

"Damn it, Owen! What the hell do you want?"

"Listen, there's not much time. You have a visitor. I outpaced her on the trail, but she's determined to see you, and I imagine she'll be along pretty soon."

"Who?"

"Some chick who's clearly not from around here."

"You left her on the trail? Why didn't you use the logging road and just drive up here to my cabin?"

"How was I supposed to give you a head's up doing that? Besides, I like to mess with the greenhorns. Makes 'em go home sooner," Owen joked giving Newt a huge grin.

"Yeah, I kinda like doing that too," Newt countered as he tried to peer around Owen's large frame. At first, he could see no one, but then the top of a tan, brimmed hat came into view followed by the rest of the hiker who sported khaki cargo pants, a dark blue scooped neck t-shirt, and a taupe all-weather jacket. The doe-eyed girl was walking toward him, and Newt found himself unnerved by how much he'd wanted Bree from Dallas to be making this social call.

"Hey, Owen, I have a few beers stuck in the stream over there by that big rock. I wanted to keep them cool so I could enjoy a couple after I got finished with this. Want to bring back three?" Newt was trying desperately to figure out a way to get Owen gone for a few minutes.

"Depends. Is it craft or domestic?" Owen asked.

"What difference does it make? It's beer. Just go get it."

"It matters and you know it," Owen grumped as he lumbered toward the gurgling stream.

Newt gave a sigh as he watched his friend walk away and then turned to watch the woman moving closer.

Bree could see Newt now that he was standing in the full light and away from the lean-to. She was too winded from following Owen on the trail to holler, so she took off her new hat and waved it. Newt, waved back and leaned against the edge of the old cattle shed to wait for her.

"Hi, Newt! Aren't you surprised? I found you all on my own. And look, I got some nice mountain clothes." Bree turned a couple of full circles so Newt could approve of her fresh look.

The clothing itself was non-descript, but Newt still struggled to contain his arousal as he noticed how nicely she filled out the seat of the cargo pants and how the t-shirt was tight in all the right places. "Surprised all right. At least this time you found a decent escort, and I'm guessing someone knows where you are. You learn fast, Bree from Dallas."

Bree smiled, trying to hide the heat creeping into her cheeks. His praise felt good.

"So, did Owen offer to bring you, or did you just get to ride along?" Newt was fairly sure Owen was forced into coming to Newt's place as Owen rarely liked socializing outside of the Moose Mercantile.

"The store owner, I think his name's Emmett, told Owen to bring me up here to see you. I guess Owen has an order for you. I didn't know you made furniture."

"A guy's gotta have a revenue stream to stay up here. When I left my position as a game warden, I didn't want to work for the resorts, so I decided to find my own gig. What brings you back?"

"I wanted to bring you a present. You know, for rescuing me yesterday." Bree's eyes were shining.

"That's not necessary."

"But I want to." She looked down with her mouth set into a disappointed pout.

Newt noticed her look of dejection. "Sure, let's talk about it in a bit. Owen's coming back with some cold beer. Do you want one?"

"Domestic or craft?"

"Damn, there are a lot of picky people around here today. Owen asked the same thing. Craft."

"Is it an IPA?" Bree asked.

"No, too hoppy." Newt said as he offered a grimace. "It's a red ale I want to try. Interested?"

"Yes. Thank you." Bree gave a happy sigh.

Newt saw Owen emerging from the trees with the six-pack in hand and directed Bree over to a large pine tree in front of the cabin. Newt pulled the chair from the front porch and gave it to her. Then, he stepped into the house and emerged with another chair and a metal milkcrate as Owen met them in the shade of the large tree that cooled the cabin. Newt used the opener from his multi-tool and passed the open bottles to each person.

"Okay, Owen, what brings you out this way?" Newt took a thirsty gulp of his brew as he waited for the gruff reply.

"This gal here needed to find you, and I guess Emmett felt sorry for her. He told me to bring this order up to you along with the passenger." Owen handed over a sheet of paper to Newt with the specifics for the order.

"Hey, I have a name, you know," Bree challenged.

"Of course," Newt said. "Owen, this is Bree, and I want you to know that I am fine with her being here. You don't need to feel protective of my solitude."

"Sure," Owen grumbled, "but we hermits have to stick together."

"We do have to watch out for each other, but this case is an exception, Owen." Newt looked over at Bree. "Nice day, isn't it? The birdsong and the stream melody really make this beer taste good." Newt raised his bottle. Bree and Owen joined the toast which was immediately followed by silence.

Bree looked at the voiceless men and began to fidget. "Don't you guys listen to a radio or something?"

"Why?" Owen said. "Just a bunch of noise pollution."

"You're telling me you like listening to nothing?" Bree was unconvinced.

"It's not silent," Newt insisted. "Be quiet now."

No one spoke, and Bree squirmed, feeling uncomfortable with having nothing to focus on. She hated the quiet and was at a loss to understand what value the men saw in it.

Newt was the first to break the calm. "Don't you hear the birds singing and the babble of the stream and the breeze moving through the pine branches. It sounds like a whisper."

"Whatever. Sure," Bree agreed just to get the lesson to end. "I'd rather talk if it's okay with you guys."

"Of course, you would," Owen said sarcastically.

After that comment, Bree found she didn't even know how to begin a conversation. She wanted to talk, but she didn't know how to break into it. Her mind jumped to her gift for Newt. She could impress them with her find of the unusual animal on the knife's hilt.

"Newt, I really appreciate your help yesterday, and I wanted to bring you this." Bree fished the knife out of her backpack and extended her hand. "It has a really strange looking animal on it. I was hoping you might be able to show me where that animal lives."

"Well, thanks. Let's see what we have here." Newt took the knife. Looking down on the carved handle, he tried to hide his amusement as he pulled the decorative knife out of its sheath. The blade was a conversation piece and not functional. "It's beautiful, Bree, and I'm sure it's going to serve me well." Newt gave her a reassuring smile.

Bree felt a flush creep up her neck and into her cheeks. She was so happy to hear he liked the gift. "But what about the animal?" she asked.

"The animal. Well, there's a thing about the animal."

"Lemme see!" Owen demanded. Newt held the knife so his friend could look at it. "Are you serious?" he asked incredulously, staring over at Bree.

"What? What's it called? Where does it live?" She really wanted to know.

"It's called a Jackalope, and it's a hoax," Owen answered as if she should already know the answer.

"A hoax?" Bree struggled to hold back her tears.

"Yeah, it was a taxidermy trick from the 1930s. Someone got the great idea to put antelope horns on a jackrabbit. The joke started in Wyoming and eventually migrated to Colorado as a staple in tourist traps."

"Oh." Bree looked down feeling idiotic. Her face turned red with embarrassment since she'd wanted to make a stellar impression on Newt. She hoped to please him, and now she looked like a foolish child who didn't know anything.

"It's a nice blade, Bree, and it'll remind me to look for the wonders and miracles of nature." Newt tried to sound reassuring. "You see them all the time 'round here if you care to notice them. Miracles and wonders, not Jackalopes."

"Yeah, like finding a clueless city dweller in the middle of the wilderness," Owen chimed in.

"Something like that," Newt replied, shooting dagger eyes at his friend.

Bree was uncomfortable and uncertain about what to do next. She decided to focus on a diversion and try erasing her beer breath. She unzipped the front pocket of her pack, pulled out a stick of gum, unwrapped it, stuffed the minty goodness into her mouth and dropped the wrapper on the ground.

Both men immediately froze, fury crossing their faces.

"Is she for real, man? Who just drops trash on the ground like that?" Owen said as he looked over to see Newt's reaction.

"Oh, she's for real all right, and clearly needs to be taught a thing or two about being respectful."

Bree, not understanding what she did or why they were clearly upset with her, cast her gaze between both men with a quizzical look on her face. Seeing Newt's hard expression, his obsidian eyes and furrowed brow, made her feel like she had a rock in her belly.

Newt's flinty gaze was not lost on Owen who knew social time was over. The girl was going to get a serious talking to at the very least, and there was no sense in his getting involved. Without excusing himself, Owen stood up, put his empty beer bottle next to the others and simply walked away.

Chapter 5

Newt watched Owen's lumbering form disappear and waited until he was sure his friend was well on his way back to his truck. Then, Newt stood up.

"Bree, we need to have a discussion about a few things now that you are here." Newt held his hand out to her and pulled her to her feet. "Let's go sit on the porch and enjoy the shade while we have a little chat," he said, taking her small hand and leading her toward the cabin.

Bree trailed behind him, feeling bewildered and a little bit curious about what he was going to say. Newt sat down on the porch's edge and patted the space next to him. Bree took a shy step toward him and perched daintily on the edge.

Newt adjusted his position to face her. "You've come back. Is delivering your thank-you gift the *only* reason you are here?"

Bree blushed and looked down at her hands. "No," she murmured.

"So, am I correct in assuming that you have been thinking about our conversation regarding the type of relationship I want with a woman I care about? Bree, please look at me."

Bree lifted her eyes to his. "Yes." She felt breathless.

"Okay, then we need to talk about our expectations. First, I will never harm you. I am your protector and your champion. I also want what is best for you, and because I care about you, I will discipline you if I see that you need it. You recall how I will discipline you, correct?"

"You will spank me." Bree's voice was a bit shaky, but she wasn't sure if it was because she was afraid of being disciplined or if she was suddenly feeling something akin to arousal.

"Yes, and I will do it because I cherish you. You can also expect that I will lavish you with my attention and kindness. I will spoil you, not with things, but with experiences and companionship. Does this sound like something you want?"

"Yes."

"Very good. Now, you are receiving your first discipline today. Because this is your first spanking, I will let you keep your britches on. However, the next time, and the times after that, I will be warming up your bare rear end. Do you understand, my sweet?"

"Yes." Bree wasn't sure she liked where the conversation was heading and squirmed.

"If what I have said is acceptable to you, I want you to stand up and lay yourself over my lap."

"Now?" Bree's voice squeaked with fresh panic.

"Yes, now." Newt patted his lap and waited.

Bree stood, looking at him with wide eyes, her feet anchored in place. He was serious. She knew it now. He was really going to spank her.

"Come on," he said patting his leg more insistently this time. "The sooner you submit, the sooner we get to do something fun."

Bree broke free of her frozen stance and reluctantly approached him. When she stood before him, he reached out and carefully lowered her across his strong, muscular legs.

Using his large forearm across her back, Newt held Bree in place. "Tell me why I am disciplining you, pet."

"Because I was disrespectful and threw trash on the ground."

"That is correct." Newt gave her rear a solid smack.

"Hey! That hurt!" Bree screeched trying to worm herself free of his tight grasp.

"It's supposed to hurt. When your sweet bottom is on fire, you'll remember today's lesson." He administered another powerful swat.

Bree tried frantically to wriggle free, but he was too strong and held her firmly. She was draped over his lap like a child. It was demeaning. "You'd better stop it. I have a lawyer, you know."

"Go ahead and call him with that cellphone of yours that doesn't work up here. I'll spank him too, and you know I can do it." He gave her another punishing swat. "You need to understand the damage flatlanders and urbanites do up here is not easily repaired. Not taking any personal responsibility for destroying what Nature has spent centuries creating hurts more than the swats I'm landing on your backside!" Newt smacked her three more times, each one more forceful than the last.

"It was a gum wrapper! You can't do this. I'm a grown woman!" Bree whimpered.

"Yes, it was a gum wrapper and it perfectly represents a careless and destructive attitude. You are a grown woman, and I expect you to act like one. Only children are careless like that until a concerned adult teaches them better." He issued another solid thwack and then another. "I care about you, Bree from Dallas. I care about the wild spaces too, and you must be taught how to act and how to leave the beautiful spaces better than you found them. Your father should have taught you about accountability and swatted your rear a long time ago." Newt again administered three more stinging swats and noticed that Bree was no longer fighting his stern hand.

"I'm sorry," she sobbed. "I am sorry."

Newt immediately stayed his hand and picked her up. He set her on her feet and turned her so he could look into her round, tear-rimmed eyes. Then, he pulled her close to him, eased her onto his lap and folded his tree-trunk arms around her. He smoothed her hair and rubbed her back with his large, capable hands as he spoke.

"I know that sweetness, but respect is the most important piece of any relationship. I respect you too much to let you get away with hurting the natural world."

"I understand." Bree snuggled her head into his chest, closed her eyes, and sighed. The importance of what Newt was saying was starting to make a little bit of sense.

"You don't yet, but you will." Newt held her for a bit then pulled her away from him and stood her up. He kissed her gently on her forehead, and gently rubbed her sore rear. He smiled just a bit when she flinched since he knew her tail end had to be red and terribly tender. He also knew she'd think twice before she was so disrespectful to the earth. She had so much to learn, and he was the man to teach her.

Chapter 6

Jessica looked at the large clock behind the check-in desk. The gold Roman numerals told her she had ten minutes left of her shift when the phone rang. Jessica growled in frustration. Jeff Johnson, her relief, had gone down the hall to the restaurant for some iced tea before he took over. She desperately hoped the call wasn't a problem she'd have to deal with. Perhaps someone had dialed a wrong number.

"Welcome to Mount Goliath Resort and Spa, the best mountain destination. This is—"

"Jessica. Yes, I know," growled an angry voice.

"Mr. Phillips. How may I help you today?" Jessica struggled not to show her initial surprise and subsequent annoyance. She couldn't catch a break today and knew from his tone this call was going to be unpleasant as well as labor intensive.

"Have you seen Breanna? I haven't been able to reach her. She needs to get home ASAP."

"Sir, she checked out yesterday."

"What! Where did she go?"

"I'm not exactly sure, sir. She asked about the man who

rescued her. I think she might have wanted to thank him for his help. Anyway, I bet she'll be home within a few days."

"You can't possibly know that and you people are completely inept. Get Ted Niven and Greg Wahl on the line."

"Sir, with all due respect, I hardly think calling in security is necessary."

"Mind your place, Jessica," he said. His voice had an unmistakable undercurrent of warning.

Jessica swallowed hard to hide her uneasiness. "Yes, sir. I'll get them on the line in the conference room straight away."

Jessica called the men on the walkies. Once the guards were assembled in the conference room, Jessica made sure Mr. Phillips was able to directly communicate with them before she quietly closed the door behind her. The clock hands showed Jessica's shift ended an hour ago. She'd put in a four-teen-hour day. Of course, there was no reward for it since her position was on salary. She informed Jeff on the nature of the conversation going on in the office and slipped away as quickly and quietly as possible. Jessica popped into the giftshop for one of the twenty-five cent ice cream cones, and scrambled to get over to her room in the employee dorms before Mr. Phillips came up with some other time consuming task he wanted her to do.

Newt was surprised by how much daylight had filtered out of the summer sky. The day had completely gotten away from him. It was nearing supper time, and he still needed to get Bree settled in for the night. He'd make further arrangements for her tomorrow, but for now, he needed to come up with an idea for some grub. He settled on ham and cheese sandwiches and would share the last of the craft beer with her. Newt gathered plates and silverware from the kitchen area and handed them to Bree.

"Please set the table. I'll have supper together in one shake of a lamb's tail."

"We're eating a lamb?" She looked horrified.

"No. That's just an expression. I meant to say I'll have dinner on the table momentarily."

Bree looked relieved as she arranged the plates and silverware. Newt couldn't help but smile. She was so innocent, and a bit silly, and absolutely adorable!

He placed a thick sandwich on each plate and went back to the kitchen to retrieve the opened beers before sitting down across from her.

Bree immediately lifted the top slice of bread and peeled the ham off the sandwich before she began eating just the cheese, bread and wild lettuce.

"That ham is related to bacon, you know." Newt tried to hide his annoyance at her wastefulness.

Bree looked up with an astonished expression. "Well, why didn't you say so?"

He chuckled in amusement as he watched her slap the cured meat back between the bread slices and attack the sandwich with gusto.

"You can sleep in my bed again tonight. In the morning, I'll make you some breakfast, and tell you what's next on our agenda. How would you like to go hiking and maybe catch a few fish?"

"Eww. Are you serious?"

"I don't kid about going fishing, Bree. We can go for a long hike through one of my favorite forests and spend the day at my secret fishing spot. I promise to let you off the hook, so to speak. Just because we go to a fishing spot doesn't mean we have to catch any fish."

"Can't we drive?"

"Sorry, sweetness. I don't own a vehicle. You'll have to hoof it."

"You don't own a car? Seriously?"

"I don't need one up here. I hike to wherever I need to go."

"How do you get your supplies?" Bree's eyes narrowed with suspicion. She wasn't going to look stupid in front of him again and kicked herself for her gullibility earlier.

"I buy craft beer and bribe Owen into delivering my supplies for me or taking my handmade furniture out of here. He's a field biologist and has that beat-up truck from the non-profit he conducts research for."

Bree looked at Newt like he'd just grown horns.

"Seriously. I don't own a vehicle, so you are going to have to power yourself wherever you want to go."

Once again Newt tucked her into his bed and wished her sweet dreams. When Bree was snuggled in, she was struck by the care he'd taken to make her comfortable before he went out to the front room. She could hear his footsteps retreat and then the loveseat springs creak when he lay down. Soon, she heard his steady breathing and knew he was asleep. Bree wished she could get to sleep so quickly, but she was having trouble getting comfortable and gingerly repositioned herself, trying not to stir up the heat in her rear. She preferred to sleep on her back, but tonight she had to lie on her side or her tummy because her backside stung like she had bees in her panties. Finding a position on her side that was tolerable, she finally settled in. For the first time ever, she heard the whispers in the pine trees that Newt had pointed out to her earlier in the day. The soft sighs sang comfort to her, and soon, Bree was lulled into a sound sleep.

The next morning, Newt made pancakes, which Bree adored, and he smiled to see her relishing them with the butter and pure maple syrup he always kept on hand. Newt liked pancakes as well, and was glad they could enjoy the simple pleasure. The rest of the day, however, went anything but smoothly. Before he could take her to the deep pool he wanted to share with her, he had to tie up some chores around the place. Newt knew the fish weren't going to bite until it got closer to dusk, but she was impatient and just wanted to get on with what she wanted to do, which was taking their hike. Bree was constantly underfoot and was making it difficult for him to get any work done. She had obviously never been in a functional and operating shop before and had no concept of where to stand while he used the saw. She wouldn't listen when he insisted she don personal protective equipment while he worked. She refused to wear the earplugs he provided and gave him trouble over wearing safety glasses.

"They aren't very cute," she complained to him.

"Fashion's not an issue up here, but having two eyes is, so put them on. Now!"

Grudgingly, she complied, but Newt wearied of having to repeat safety lectures. And while he would never do it, he had a glimpse into why people felt compelled to dump stubborn dogs at the shelter.

"I'm so bored. When can we leave?" Bree slumped against the wall while she whined and complained incessantly.

"I explained why earlier. The fish won't be out until the insects start flying. We'll go later."

Bree pushed off and spun a circle on one foot, dancing like a ballerina inside a jewelry box. "Isn't there something else we can do? I am so bored I'm about to fall over."

Newt stopped sanding the fragrant wood. "Are you

hungry? How about having lunch?"

Bree's eyes lit up. "Lunch. Yes, lunch sounds wonderful."

But then she whined about the food he made for her.

"Eggs for lunch? Don't you have some black-bean burgers or tofu dogs? Eggs aren't real lunch food," she groused.

Newt found her lack of appreciation disrespectful and annoying. There was nothing to be done for it. This bad behavior had to stop, and he was ready to put her over his knee and tan her hide right then and there.

"Bree, you are acting inappropriately and it needs to stop right now," Newt said in a no-nonsense tone.

"Oh, and you think you are going to make me behave, do you?" Bree taunted.

In one swift movement, Newt came around the table and hooked his arm around Bree's waist. Lifting her from the chair, he switched positions with her sprawled across his lap.

"What are you doing?" Bree began to struggle.

"Giving what you asked for."

"What? You can't do this. You spanked me last night, and it still hurts!"

Newt held Bree in place as he reached around her middle, unbuttoned and pulled down her cargo pants. He deftly used one hand to wrestle her pretty, lacy blue panties off too. Her shapely rear was still rosy from the night before, and he knew she was going to feel a more powerful sting this time around. He administered a hard, open-handed smack on her bare backside.

Her bottom was on fire, the conflagration rekindled from the night before. Bree struggled to get free of his tight grasp, but he was too strong and held her firmly in place. "Cut it out! I didn't deserve that." She hated feeling so helpless and was also embarrassed and a bit panicked when she realized he might be taking a good look at her personal area.

"If you want to act like a wanton child, you can expect to

be treated like one." Newt swatted her in rhythm to his words. "I will not tolerate disrespect and have reasons for doing things the way I do them. It is not your place to disrupt what I am building here, especially since the last thing you are is an expert in my world."

"But I wasn't disrespectful!" Bree set her jaw and refused to let any of her tears spill even though her backside hurt like the dickens.

Newt pulled her tightly to him, stood up and carried her to a corner by the kitchen window. "Then you will stand here with your nose to the wall and think about how your behavior can't be defined as disrespectful." He stood her up on her feet and turned her to the wall.

"Fine! I'm not giving you the satisfaction!" She spun around in fury and settled herself into the corner before she tried pulling her bottoms up.

Newt stopped her hands. "No. You stand here just as you are. When you are ready to apologize and accept the rest of your punishment, please speak up. Until then, not one word."

Bree bit the inside of her cheek and railed at the injustice of what he was expecting her to do. Minutes passed, but the heat in her backside did not dissipate. She turned her head around to see if Newt had left the room. No such luck. He looked at her with a stern expression and motioned for her to look back at the wall. She turned her face back to the corner and sighed heavily. It was so unfair that he placed her in such an embarrassing position, but Bree was unable to keep the flames of indignation burning for long and began to think about what he had told her. There was no doubt about it, she had been rude and churlish. She would have never acted like that with the staff in Dallas, and as Bree reflected on it, she knew she was in the wrong. Plainly, Newt wasn't changing his mind, so if she wanted to get out of the corner, she was going to have to make the first move.

She tried to smooth the edge out of her voice. "Okay. I'm sorry."

"I see." Newt's voice no longer held a stern edge. "Sorry for what?"

"For being ungrateful and disrespectful."

"Then, my sweet, you may leave the corner. Please come lie across my lap for the rest of your punishment."

"The rest? I thought we were done." Bree's voice broke as she realized he was serious about continuing.

"I told you what happens to ungrateful girls and that I would finish with your spanking when you left the corner. Come on, now. Let's tie this up."

Bree sighed and shuffled toward him, her pants and panties pooled around her ankles. Newt gently helped her lie back over his lap. "Five more swats. I want to be sure you remember this is not how to treat others, especially the person who is most interested in your well-being. From here on, you will address me as Sir when I discipline you. Understand?"

"Yes."

"Yes, what?"

"Yes, Sir."

"Very well. Five more and we are done." He landed five more solid swats on the tender tops of her thighs.

Bree inhaled quickly and held her breath. She couldn't see how it could sting any more than it already was. Somehow, he found a way to make it happen. She whimpered, trying to keep the floodgates closed, but her tears spilled over as he stood her on her feet and let her collapse into his arms.

"I'm sorry I complained about lunch." She struggled with a catch in her throat and began to gulp for air. And, as she cried, she felt worse about how she'd behaved. It occurred to her that she might have been awful enough for him to send her away. Bree began crying even harder.

Newt looked at her now with concern in his eyes and could

see she was unable to hold in her sadness. Tears were streaming down her face, and he held her tighter.

"I don't want to go home!" she sobbed. "I can't go back there now that I know about this place, and now that I know about you!"

He watched her, and his heart melted with her tears. She was so adorable and lost, and he genuinely wanted to help her. "I didn't say anything about your having to go home. Tell me what you want sweet one," he said with a soft voice filled with comfort.

"I don't know what I want!" she wailed.

Newt could see she was like a toddler who needed a nap but wouldn't succumb to sleep for fear of missing something interesting. He held her like the injured child she was, the one he was beginning to see inside of her. She burrowed her head beneath his chin and relaxed into him as he swayed with her and soothed her. "It's okay, pet. Most people don't know what they want."

Bree looked up at him. "Really?" She was hiccupping now.

"From what I've seen, most folks spend their entire lives trying to figure out how to live true to themselves." Newt helped her stand up and gently pulled her panties up over her hips and then pulled up her pants and fastened them. He set her in the chair and then kneeled before her, brushing the tears from her face, he looked her in the eyes. "If you are ready to listen to me and do what I say, I will take you on our outing now. This will happen only if you pay attention and heed what I say," his voice was stern, yet caring.

Bree's eyes lit up. "I will! I promise." She reached out and hugged him tightly.

He smiled and hugged her back harder.

Chapter 7

Ted Niven and Greg Whal didn't have an easy time tracking the boss' daughter since the cooperation of the locals was paltry at best. After the phone conference with Mr. Phillips, both men found Jessica and brought her into the office for questioning.

If security was involved, Jessica knew playing dumb was the best bet to keep herself out of trouble. She wasn't stupid and knew instinctively there was nothing good to come for Breanna if these men were asking questions. Jessica liked Breanna and wasn't about to rat the poor girl out.

"We understand you spoke to Breanna yesterday. Where did she go?" Ted Niven's heavy eyebrows, square jaw and forehead made her think of the old Dick Tracy comics. *Just the facts, ma'am.*

"I have no idea where she went." Jessica was noncommittal.

"We know she talked to you. What did she want?" Niven was already annoyed.

"She wanted to know where her knight in shining armor

came from. I told her he was most likely from a nearby canyon."

"Which one, Jessica?"

"I can't remember. You know there are tons of guys in the backcountry. I don't know many of them, so how should I be expected to keep them straight?" She was pleasant, yet she was quite aware of how infuriatingly elusive she was answering their questions, offering only vague facts about her conversation with Breanna.

She saw Niven's jaw tighten as he looked over at Whal.

"Need I remind you that no one, Jessica, *no one* is irreplaceable," the silver-haired Whal said in a strict, fatherly voice. "We need more information, so stop playing with us."

Better not push it too far. "I really don't know which guy it was. I didn't see much of him because I was helping Breanna before the guy left. You can ask Justin from the rescue team who the guy is. I was never in contact with Breanna's escort. I just figure he has to be from one of the nearby canyons because he walked her back over here the next day."

"From which direction?" Niven was clearly finding the questioning tedious.

"I'm not sure. When I saw them, they were in the big meadow. They could have come in from any direction other than west." Jessica leaned back in her chair and crossed her arms.

"Anything else?" Niven already knew the answer.

"Not that I can think of," Jessica said brightly. "Now, may I please be excused?"

"Get out of here," Niven growled. The woman somehow managed to tell them very little about who they were looking for.

Jessica stood up and left the room, closing the office door behind her.

"Damn locals," grumped Niven. "I've never seen a less cooperative demographic in my life."

"They do look out for each other, but we'll find her." Whal's voice was assured. "Mr. Phillips moved his event back a week and is out of town with other potential clients. It should give us plenty of time to find her. There can't be too many canyons within a day's walk." Whal gathered the notes he'd taken from the phone conversation and opened the office door. "Come on, Ted, let's go. I have a topographical map in my office. It won't take long to narrow things down."

After packing a light snack and filtered water, Newt took Bree's hand and escorted her on their adventure. Her behavior had vastly improved, and he was enjoying her company. Newt was proud of her for moving past her tantrum and demonstrating she was willing to let him teach her, and he was eager to open the wonders of his world to her.

She followed him willingly as he led her to the stream on his property, they walked along the water's edge and into a grove of trees. He showed her a slow-moving area where a deep pool formed. Rocks naturally lay flat and over the water forming a narrow shelf, and Newt carefully steered her to the bank's edge.

"Take off your boots and socks," he said as he began to unlace his own and set them back from the edge of the stone overhang, with his socks inside. Bree didn't question him. She unlaced her boots, took off her socks, and set them beside his. Again, he took her hand and led her toward a low area on the bank. Letting go of her hand, he sucked in his breath, and plunged his bare feet into the icy glacier runoff. Bree stood on the bank looking confused.

"Your turn," he said, smiling and extending his hand to her.

"What? You want me to put my feet in there?" Bree took a few steps back.

"Yes. Trust me. You'll see." Newt smiled reassuringly.

Bree felt the warmth of his encouragement and responded by putting herself into his care. She cautiously approached the water's edge.

"This water comes straight from the glaciers above Summit Lake. Come on in, the water's fine once your feet go numb."

Bree stepped into the creek and stood stock still, eyes wide.

"Now, clear your mind and listen to the sound of the water moving and feel how it's speaking to you. Can't you feel it loves you?"

Standing in the frigid water, Bree was convinced that she wouldn't get her feet warmed up until a year from July. Still, she tried to do as he asked and felt the sway of the water as it moved within its etched out rut of the banks and eddy around her feet. The water felt alive. It rocked and reassured her. She couldn't help but smile. Bree had never taken the time to intentionally stand still before.

"See what I mean?"

"Yes." She looked up, a sense of wonder erasing the worry lines that were etched in her beautiful face before she communed with the stream.

They spent the rest of the afternoon sitting on the stone outcropping above the deep pool. Newt helped Bree distinguish differences among the birdsongs and pointed out the different pine species. She'd never seen so many interesting things, and the more aware she became of them, the more she noticed the varieties of the trees and their different shapes, sizes and colors. She was just getting ready to ask Newt a question about pinecones, when he suddenly shook his head and tilted it to indicate she shouldn't speak and ought to look across the stream. Bree's eyes followed his direction, just in time to see a Mule deer. The doe moved through the brush with a spotted fawn following closely behind her. The doe nosed through the undergrowth completely unconcerned as she daintily pulled leaves from a Bearberry bush. Bree watched, enthralled. Newt watched Bree's sense of childlike wonder and found himself taken by her loveliness. In the quiet, time seemed to sit down to join them, and the light began to fade as the sun started to slip behind the highest peak. The peacefulness stayed with the couple long after the doe and fawn had moved on.

They stopped by the section of stream where the beer was chilling, and Newt grabbed four more before he and Bree walked back to his cabin. Once inside, he began pulling canned beans, jarred salsa, flour, baking powder, salt, and lard along with eggs from the kitchen storage. The sun had long ago disappeared behind the ridge, and as darkness set in, so did the chill. Bree pulled her jacket from her pack and settled back into her chair, eager to find out what Newt would do next. She watched him open two of the red ales and hand one to her. She marveled at how much had changed in such a short time and watched as Newt, once again, made sure she was well cared for. Bree took a deep drink of the ale and noticed the alcohol went straight to her head and warmed her belly. What melted her heart was how relaxed and safe she felt in the powerful man's tiny kitchen. She was content to stay exactly where she was, right here with Newt.

The big man moved through the small kitchen area like a master chef. Newt filled a teakettle and turned on the heat underneath it, poured a can of pinto beans in chili sauce into a pan and set it on another burner to heat. He threw the flour, salt, and baking powder together and then using a fork, he began folding lard, that he scooped from a lidded glass dish, into the dry ingredients. Newt made sure he didn't mention the lard since it was an animal product. Mixing in small amounts of warm water, Newt created a dough, which he formed into balls. He proceeded to flatten them one at a time with the bottom of a dinner plate. His sizable cast-iron skillet was hot, greased, and ready when Newt threw the flattened dough onto the hot surface. Before Bree knew it, Newt created a stack of fresh tortillas and was frying eggs.

Grabbing two deep camping plates, Newt ladled beans onto the plates and slid the eggs on top and plopped generous spoonsful of salsa on top. He folded two warm tortillas in half and then half again before setting a plate in front of Bree and another on the opposite corner of the table. He turned and pulled a jar of homemade salsa from the cupboard, grabbed two spoons, and threw a clean dishtowel over the tortilla stack before he opened the second pair of beers.

"Be a good girl. Start eating and don't wait for me, I'll be right back. I need to run outside to get my chair."

Bree did as she was told and immediately began to taste the food he'd prepared for her. She was famished. Lunch time seemed so long ago. Newt returned shortly, just in time to find Bree shoveling an unladylike heaping spoon of beans into her mouth.

"Good?" he asked as he put his second chair by the other place setting. She nodded. And he smiled. "I waited until your mouth was full to ask. I get fewer complaints that way." Newt sat down and began attacking his own plate. "I see that eggs are okay for dinner now."

"Gosh, this is delicious!"

"The mountain air has a way of making nearly everything taste good. I'm not much of a cook you know. I'm more of an assembler. I know how to make foods match up and can put pantry staples together to make them pass as a nice meal. My ability in mountain culinary skills, however, seems to get undeserved recognition because everything tastes better up here."

"Does food taste better when you are on the trail?"

"Especially when you're on the trail!" Newt chirped and then smiled broadly. He continued with passion, "When you're hiking all day underneath the weight of a pack, you could eat tree bark and think it was a delight."

Bree smiled at his enthusiasm.

"Which brings me to the next order of business. I want to give you a guided tour of some remote areas I know." Newt captured her hands in his. "It would mean so much to me if I could show you more of this place."

"Don't you have to work? Owen said you have a new order to get ready for someone."

"That's the beauty of craftsmanship. The custom pieces get done when they are done. There's no rushing creativity and craft. What do you say, Bree from Dallas? Are you ready to be my mountain novice? It will be an adventure. I promise."

Bree was swept along by his zeal and giddy with anticipation. She also felt the unmistakable heat of arousal begin to burn through her. The fire that was warming her feelings for him was creating the flames she felt down low and they were taking her over. Her arousal was filling her mind with steamy images of herself and Newt naked and entwined in each other's grasp. Her mind flitted back to his punishment earlier that day, and Bree found herself wanting him even more. She blushed shamelessly.

"Are you, okay?" Newt noticed the intense look that came over her and thought she might be running a fever.

"Oh, yes," Bree said, fanning herself with an open hand.

"I guess I just got a little bit warm now that we're inside and my tummy is full."

He was relieved. She was feeling okay and he had to admit when the color filled her cheeks, he found her simply stunning. "Well then, I suppose we should turn in. You get my bed again. I'll sleep out in the front room."

Bree started to protest, but Newt waved her to silence.

"We'll start out early in the morning. We have to be on the trail shortly after sunup this time of year to avoid those monsoon rains like you were caught in when I first found you." Newt stood up from the table. "Come on, I'll get you settled in, and we'll sally forth in the morning."

Bree followed him to the small room at the back of the cabin. Once again, he tucked her safely underneath flannel sheets and a heavy quilt. Newt stood backlit in the doorway and said, "Sweet dreams, my pet," before he turned to walk down the hallway.

Bree called him back. "Thank you for taking me to see the deer and the water, and for the wonderful dinner."

"You are most welcome, and I'm glad you enjoyed it. Get to sleep. We are leaving at dawn."

Newt turned to leave, and before too long, Bree heard him settle onto the loveseat. The cabin was quiet, and she reflected on how her debutante life in Dallas seemed years away from her now.

Chapter 8

Bree woke to the morning chill when there was still no light to escort the dawn into the area where Newt had built his home. She shivered and leaned over the side of his bed to draw her pack toward her and fished out her spare pair of wool socks, slipped them over her frozen toes, and tried to get back to sleep. It didn't work. She kept trying to warm herself, but her thoughts kept suggesting she'd only warm up if Newt was beside her. She created a vision of him holding her, comforting her, protecting her, and then caressing her. Bree let the fantasy play out in her mind; her body didn't know the difference between an imagined and actual encounter. Bree felt hot and moist between her legs, and shameless. She hoped Newt would take her not just into the mountains, but also into other unknown territories and smiled when she let her mind consider those adventures. She was breathless and became even more aroused.

"Are you okay?" Newt asked. He stood, slightly backlit, in the doorway of his bedroom.

Startled, Bree sat straight up and gave him a panicked stare, looking like she'd been caught stealing cookies.

"Are you having trouble breathing? The altitude can present trouble to people who aren't used to it." His voice was edged with concern.

"No. Not at all. I was envisioning our trip today and trying to clear my head with some deep breathing exercises," Bree lied and felt guilty for it.

"If that's what you call deep breathing, then we're in serious trouble. Trust me, you are going to find out what deep breathing is. Some of the switchbacks on the trails we travel today are pretty wicked if you aren't in decent shape."

The word 'wicked' made Bree smile.

"Get yourself ready to go. Here's a larger pack you can borrow. You're gonna need it." Newt tossed a tan, internal-frame pack into the dimly lit room. Bree caught it by a shoulder strap.

"Pack your extra clothes and sunscreen if you have it. Did you bring a flashlight with you? If not, I'll lend you one. You should have plenty of room left over, so bring the pack out to the kitchen and we'll load it up with other supplies." Newt turned to leave and called over his shoulder, "We'll have some steel-cut oats with canned milk and nuts. Carbs and protein— the breakfast of champions!"

Bree was amazed the simple meal could be so filling and realized she'd let her strict eating habits go all to hell since she'd been with Newt. Her organic, gluten-free, sugar-free, fat-free, whole food, locally-supplied diet was now miles behind her. Life in Dallas was predictable and afforded her much control over her day-to-day existence. She quickly realized she was starting not to care about any of that anymore and was surprised to find herself becoming less rigid as she learned to be open to trying new things. Around Newt, she couldn't get away with being a picky eater like she had been at home. Having her way about things like food choices wasn't important to her anymore. What mattered was being with Newt and her desire to please him.

The lavender dawn was just beginning to filter into the sky above the ridgeline when they hit the trail to the Mount Goliath Natural Area. Newt loaded her pack before they left his cabin, and because this was her first trek, he packed her light. She was still lagging far enough behind him on the trail that he had to pull up to wait for her.

"I think this pack weighs a hundred pounds," Bree grumped no more than a half mile into their trek.

"You'd best count yourself lucky that I carry the really heavy stuff."

"I don't understand why we have to bring so many clothes and a bunch of extra stuff that we already have enough of. We have a lot of water, and it's heavy. Why can't we just drink from the streams and lakes?"

"First of all, I am the expert out here, not you. We have to wait for the water to filter since you can't count on being able to drink from fresh sources. You haven't tasted water after it's been treated with iodine or chlorine dioxide, which works too, but it's disgusting until you get used to it. I brought some powdered electrolyte drink mix to make the treated water more palatable. For the hike, it's just easier to bring fresh water with us." Newt changed the subject. "Look around at the beauty of this place."

Bree did, and all she could see was the steep trail ahead of her with no visible escape from the crevice they were climbing up. "If it's so beautiful, why are you carrying that giant sidearm and a shotgun? You could carry more of this stuff if you didn't have an arsenal on you."

He tried not to sound exasperated with her grumping.

"Sweetness, this is bear country. Since bears don't always act predictably, I must be prepared."

"Fine, it's bear country." Bree exhaled heavily. She didn't believe it for a minute. The trail was steep and deeply rutted. She looked down at her boots as she took one step and then another. She used her hands to pull the pack's shoulder straps away from the soreness in her shoulders created by the weight of the pack hanging off her back. Bree just knew the walking would go on *forever*.

"Just a little farther. There's a wide area coming up where we can take a break and have a snack. I'll fill you in on a few wilderness-safety practices you need to become aware of and use."

"You're with me. What else do I need?"

"I want to keep you safe. One of the challenges to enjoying the wilderness is to be prepared for the unforeseen, and we may not always be together. Nature, unlike some urban center, doesn't have traffic lights and rules that everyone is expected to follow."

"Fine." But Bree didn't mean fine as in all was well. She meant fine with an impatient snarky edge to it. Newt took note of it.

It seemed to Bree that the short distance Newt predicted before they got to take their break went on for about eight more miles. She was preparing to mock him about his sense of distance when he motioned for her to follow him off the trail and into an area where rocks and gravel created a clearing. Nearby was a tree that was still standing but looked to be cut in half vertically.

"What happened to that tree?" Bree asked as she followed Newt over to a grouping of low boulders.

"Lightning hit it. You don't want to mess around with lightning up here. Get down and to cover immediately or risk being the tallest thing in the area. I've had a few near misses but have never been a lightning rod. Owen has. He's terrified of it and will bivouac on the trail if he hears thunder or sees any flashes in the sky." Newt set his pack next to the rocks, and then seated himself comfortably on top of them as he pulled a water bottle free from a mesh side pocket of his pack.

"Bivouac?" Bree followed suit, set her pack down, parked her rear on a rock and retrieved her water bottle.

"That's when you improvise a temporary camp or shelter. I've seen Owen set a record for assembling a tent in the middle of a trail. He was so panicked he broke an important rule of backwoods etiquette by obstructing a right of way. Owen's a stickler for the rules, but when it comes to lightning, anything goes."

"Are there are a lot of rules out here? It seems to be just like in Dallas: don't tuck your jeans into ankle boots or wear a vintage piece of clothing without something modern."

"Uhm, sure. Except these rules are about safety and creating a terrific experience, so everyone can enjoy the area."

"And you don't think fashion is about enjoying a view?" Bree said, looking indignant.

"It's just not the view we go for up here," Newt responded then smiled. "You're messing with me, right?"

"Right. I'm starting to feel like Dallas is on another planet."

"I think you'll find that the longer you are in nature, the farther away and more alien being an urban dweller becomes. I didn't start out here and had a lot to learn about how to live at ease in the wild. I learned respect from my hard lessons, but I believe I'm better for it."

A veil of clouds crossed in front of the sun in an otherwise clear sky, taking the heat from the air and making the rocks feel warm and welcoming. Newt slid over next to Bree, put his arm around her and pulled her close. She leaned into him and rested her head on his chest.

"So safe," she said and sighed.

"Yes, sweet girl. Listen to me, and I'll keep you safe."

―――――――

The break did them wonders, and they returned to the trail feeling rested. Bree settled into the rigor of packing what she needed to survive in the wild. The load was heavy, the trail was steep, the hike was grueling, but Bree discovered she was enjoying the challenge.

Eventually, they neared the top of the rise they had hiked toward the entire morning. Bree could see the tops of the trees as they travelled. The pines seemed to touch the sky even though the trunks were set into the rocky ground of the ridgetop. When she and Newt reached those trees, Bree was unprepared for the magnificence of what lay before her. She could see for miles! A far blue peak kissed the sky while it snuggled in behind four other peaks in the foreground. They were covered with blue tinted treetops. The two furthest peaks had trees only partway up the mountainsides. Baren rock and large white spots were at the top of the tallest points. Bree imagined herself as a giant, using the four mountain tops to jump over to the barren peak. They had just spent hours climbing out of the basin where Newt lived, and Bree imagined it would take weeks to get to the farthest mountaintop.

―――――――

Newt slowed his pace and waited. He wanted to see Bree's expression when she topped the rise. She stood next to the trees and observed the horizon, and Newt was sure he heard her gasp. He knew she wouldn't find words for the beauty of it. He gave her time to take it all in and then watched as she turned back to him, the light of astonishment fresh on her lovely face.

"You see what I mean? Now, you're beginning to understand." Newt closed the gap between them, took her hand, pulled her close, and folded his strong arms around her. Newt, the solitary, was standing there with another human being, and he was enjoying it. Nothing could have felt more right.

Chapter 9

Ted Niven and Greg Whal remained in the unmarked resort pickup, frustrated by how the store proprietor and the local were tight lipped about Breanna Phillips' whereabouts. Both security guards could clearly see the BMW rental car parked outside of the mercantile, but when the resort employees inquired about the young woman, they were met with questioning looks and vague answers.

"I just don't get it," said Whal. "Why do you suppose they don't share information about anyone?"

"I think there's inherent mistrust of outsiders. The way these places have been built up and the resulting influx of tourists and people moving in, no doubt, contributes. Lots of folks are simply priced out of their property."

"That's not our problem," said Whal.

"Really, it is. You and I can't afford to live up here and have to rely on the housing as part of our compensation at work. Face it, Ted, the Rocky Mountains are becoming a playground for the very wealthy, and the locals may think were speculators."

"Sure. Meanwhile, what do we do to find the girl?"

"I bought an area hiking map in that store. We can look at boundaries of private land and go from there. The residents are sparse right now since most of them are snowbirds and have flown the coop for the season." Niven unfolded the map and looked it over. "There's a logging road not far from here. Let's see if there's a cabin back in the area that's clearly occupied all year. I suspect there is, and I have a hunch that's where we will find our girl."

Bree and Newt hiked down the ridge they had laboriously ascended in the morning, walking once again through the Bristlecone pines that lined the trail. Newt knew they would soon leave the forest and hike along a cliff for a while. From their vantage point, they could see out across the basin where a meadow the size of three professional football fields sprawled across the valley floor. A lake lay at the bottom of the far ridge and offered hospitality to weary hikers. The place was inviting and welcomed them to set up camp, which is exactly what Newt planned to do. There was a lovely bunch of trees near the lake which he visited regularly. It was a secluded space most visitors to the area never noticed. Newt was careful to keep it that way and fastidiously left no traceable path into it although he came here often.

"Look across the valley. See the lake?" Newt said as he stepped up behind Bree, leaning in close to her, his head next to hers. He extended his arm to point out the place. "That's where we're going. It's one of my favorite places to go to be quiet, to think, to just be."

"It looks so far away." Bree's eyes were wide with wonder. "I didn't know the Mountains had fields as big as that."

"Now you see why it's so easy to get lost. These areas are much bigger than you think if you don't have any experience with wild spaces. We should get to the lake around three o'clock and the going is easy from here. The meadow is mostly flat. It'll be like walking in Texas, only prettier." Newt smiled when he saw her look up at him. A grin was playing on her lips; she looked so beautiful.

Bree was surprised at how much her knees ached once they came off the mountainside and began walking through the lush meadow grass.

"I should have worked out more before I came here. My hike from the resort didn't hurt like this one has," she complained.

"Your knees are the shock absorbers for your body as you walked down the trail, and you have the load you're carrying. The extra weight puts more force behind your balance as well as your ability to brake. You'll work into the conditioning. I'm surprised you aren't having breathing problems given the air is much thinner up here than it is in Dallas."

"I think I had time to get used to the air before I met you. I was in Denver a full week before I came to the resort."

They were walking through the lush grasses beside each other.

"What did you do for a week in Denver?" Newt asked.

"Oh, I shopped a lot. I went to a play, the zoo, and the art museum. I mostly shopped, but it wasn't as fun as I thought it would be. The stores weren't that different from the ones at home, so it was quite boring. Also, I was by myself, and shopping is never as fun when I go solo."

"You're right. That doesn't sound very enjoyable. What about seeing this place?" Newt swept his arm across her view of the meadow. He turned a full circle, to include the ridges both ahead and behind them and the dome of blue sky above. "Do you think this is fun?"

"I feel amazed. I feel curious. I also feel small and unsure of myself here. Enjoyable, yes, but I'm not sure I'd call it fun."

"Once you get more comfortable, you'll start to enjoy the challenges, and then you'll call it fun."

Bree smiled, grateful that he was taking such good care of her.

"Come on, if we get into the marshy areas near the willows, we may see some moose. Stay close to me and do not, under any circumstances, approach them. Moose are big, cranky, and often unpredictable. It is easy to get seriously hurt —or worse."

Newt held his hand out to her, and they walked together toward the lake, crossing over a thin stream that fed a marshy area where Bree could see cattails. The birdsong bounced around the wetland and could cheer any heavy heart. Newt pointed out the song of an American Dipper *cheep, che-ep, cheep, che-ee-ep*. A Redwing Black Bird that was out of its usual territory sang *cherreeur, cherreeur*.

Bree had never noticed the richness of the world around her, and each experience bordered on the exotic. How had she never taken the time to listen to birds and notice how differently they warbled? Bree wasn't sure she had ever tuned into a single bird's utterance before now.

Following along the edge of the marsh, Newt pointed out a moose cow in the distance. From their vantage point, Bree could see that the animal was much taller than the quarter horses she'd seen in the rodeos back home. The moose was close enough for Bree to see the dark chocolate colored cow's large leaf-shaped ears, humped shoulders and sparce beard that hung down between her chin and lower lip.

"I'm glad she's in the distance. She may have a calf with

her, and the last thing we want to do is get between her and her tyke."

"Agreed. She sure is amazing."

———

At last, Newt led Bree to the shore of the shallow lake. They'd take a short break before going into the trees to set up camp. While lakeside, Bree marveled at the water's clarity and pointed out several large fish happily loitering and lazily coasting in the open water.

"At least one of those guys will be tomorrow's dinner." Newt's eyes lit up with anticipation, but when he turned to look at Bree, he was disappointed and slightly irked to see her nose crinkled up and her lips formed into a grimace.

"Eww! You seriously think I'm going to eat that?" Revulsion oozed from her voice.

"I think you'll eat about anything I put in front of you. Up to now, I've been mindful of your food preferences and worked with them to help your gut transition to what's available out here. Please understand, my sweet, you simply cannot afford to be picky out here. Options are fewer and often have immediate expiration dates. Storage choices are limited. Sometimes refrigeration isn't an option."

"But you have power and a fridge at your cabin," Bree offered.

"I do, but it's all based on generators, and sometimes I have to conserve energy. I still rely on old-fashioned methods from time to time. For instance, I have a cache I use whenever I have to store a large batch of perishables."

"Can't you grow your own food?"

"I can grow a bit of it, but a large harvest just doesn't happen at this altitude. The growing season is incredibly short up here. We can get snow all year 'round. Sometimes summer doesn't come until the end of June, and sometimes winter begins near the end of August. Nature decides that, and we have to learn how to work with it."

"Can't you pick nuts and berries and stuff?" Bree desperately tried to present other options to facing a dead fish on her dinner plate.

"Again, it depends. If you are in a national forest, like we are now, there are most likely restrictions. Also, the wildlife eats those same foods you are picking for yourself. Do you want to take the dinner from, for example, that moose?"

"Gosh, I hadn't thought about that."

"Most people don't, but I'm here to show you how things work so you can be confident and enjoy your time in the wild. While you are in my care, you *will* eat what you are served. Trust me, pet. It won't be as awful as you're imagining."

Chapter 10

Newt's favorite camping spot behind the trees had a fire ring made out of stones, and he was relieved to see it just as he'd left it a few weeks back. When Bree followed him through the trees and entered the clearing, she saw a magical place and fully expected to see a unicorn by the rocks forming a wall at the back of the area. Bree imagined a storyteller with a long white beard entertaining the faeries and gnomes of the woods with a tale of a heroic adventure. She felt like a little girl and remembered how she was always seeing imaginary horses on the playground.

Newt watched her face light up as they entered the glen. Seeing her so happy and delighted was the most important thing to him. He wanted Bree to cherish and enjoy the wild places just as he cherished and enjoyed her.

They dropped their gear at the campsite, and Newt gave Bree a list of items to fish out of the packs. He watched as she dutifully pulled out the cooking pot, mess kits, and eating utensils just like he'd asked. Newt gathered firewood nearby. As he bent down to pick up some deadwood, he thought about how much he was looking forward to the ambiance of the fire. He wanted to hold Bree while they watched the dancing flames. "You carry the water filter and the cooking pot. He walked up to Bree with his arms laden with firewood. "I'll drop this wood by the pit on our way to the lake." Newt started walking, and Bree happily trotted after him. A short while later, they were standing near the water.

"It looks so clear." Bree could easily see the tan bottom of the lake.

"It's swimming with microbes and will make you wish you could die rather than have the bacteria coursing through your system. That's why we have the filter."

"I'm so glad I'm here with you. I'd never be safe out here. I can't believe how much there is to know."

"You are a clever girl and need to quit underestimating yourself. I'm proud of how well you have caught onto things today. And you look cute in those hiking boots and cargo pants. I'd say you're a natural." He smiled and then confessed, "The pun is intended."

Bree cast her eyes down and then looked back up at Newt, an attractive blush creeping onto her cheeks.

"Come on, my sweet. I'm hungry enough to eat a bear by myself, and we still have a few things to do before we can start cooking."

Bree's shirt and cargo pants were soaked after she walked back to the campsite with the cooking pot. Newt had cautioned her to fill it only half full, but Bree decided more was better, only to find that more just meant her clothes were soaked.

Newt noticed her shivering. "Go get your jacket while I get this started," he said while he assembled the combustible materials inside the fire ring. Bree gratefully set the pot down on the ground and scooted over to the tent. By the time she returned with a dry shirt and her jacket, he had coaxed the kindling into bright, frolicking flames. A fallen tree bare of bark lay near the fire and served as seating. Bree gratefully took a place next to the heat while he worked.

Her voice edged with excitement, Bree asked, "What culinary delight are you making for us tonight?"

"My famous first-night-out entrée." He had water heating in the pan as he opened two cans of beef stew and set them directly on top of a metal grate. The plates from their mess kits served as lids to hold in the heat and also kept the food warm until he dished it up. The aroma of the warming stew made her stomach growl loudly. She didn't know she was so hungry!

Newt heard her belly begging to be fed. "Patience, my sweet. This will be worth the wait."

The water boiled and Newt added a bag of dried noodles to the pot. "The secret for this meal is to use the indirect heat of the grate to boil the water. *Do not* cook noodles directly over an open flame. You'll end up with gelatinous mush. I ruined my dinner that way once. I was so hungry and nearly wanted to cry."

"You? Cry?" Bree couldn't believe him.

"Hey, I have disasters too. I'm navigating and learning from this crazy world same as everyone else. I may have more experience than many folks. And being bigger and tougher helps, but I'm still human. I was damn hungry." Newt looked at her with feigned offense.

"Of course, I'm sorry to have indicated I ever thought otherwise."

"Don't give it a second thought and prepare yourself for a culinary delight!"

Newt drained the noodles and piled them into the mess kit bowls. He used an old towel to pull the lidded stew cans from the grate and spooned generous portions into the bowls.

"Beef stroganoff," he said triumphantly as he handed a bowl to Bree, which she gratefully took.

"I'm so hungry, I don't care if the word beef is in it."

"Not just the word. Beef really is in it. Give it a try. I think you are in for a nice surprise."

Bree took a tentative bite, and to her astonishment, she liked it! She looked at Newt, her eyes round with disbelief.

"I told you food tastes better out here. Magical, isn't it?"

Bree nodded happily and turned her attention back to her quickly disappearing portion. "I hope there's seconds," she chirped.

"Don't worry. I doled this out so we could both have another portion." He looked at her and smiled. "Didn't know that I was a mind reader, did you?"

"Besides reading my mind, how'd you know I'd want more?"

"Everyone is starving after a day like today. Even though this is an easy trip, the fresh air and exertion makes a person very hungry and tired too. I'm certain you're going to sleep very well tonight."

Bree looked at the fire. "I'm sure I will. I'm not afraid to be sleeping way out here in the middle of nowhere since I feel safer than I've ever been when I'm with you."

Bear-proofing the campsite was the next order of business after supper.

"We don't sleep by this fire ring since it's where we cook. I'll build another fire near the tent to keep us company and deter marauding beasties. We'll change out of these clothes and put them in the bear bag overnight."

They carried the clean dishes and cookware to their packs, and Bree tucked the items they'd used away until the morning.

Newt put the food and toiletries into an incredibly heavy plastic bag.

"Are you sure we need to worry about real bears?" Bree looked increasingly concerned as Newt guided her through the evening's preparations.

"I have the firearms for a reason. I haven't seen any evidence of bear in the area, but you always need to be mindful. Bears can't see very well at night and are shy by nature, so it's unlikely we will encounter one tonight. If they smell us, and not food, bears will just move on."

Bree was smoothing on hand lotion, and Newt reached out with an open hand. "I need to put that in here."

"Why do I have to put my lotion in that bag?"

"To eliminate all evidence of food just in case a bear comes by looking for a little snack. Don't eat in your sleeping bag or smuggle food, gum, mints or anything like that into your tent. Put that stuff in the bear bag along with your toiletries."

"Do bears like soap?" Bree eyed him warily. He had to be teasing her.

"Love it or at least the smell of it, so you need to wash that lotion off before too long. I usually go hobo and clean myself with the white ash from the burned-out campfire. Since I don't know you all that well yet, I thought maybe we could take ash baths on our second date."

Bree eyed him suspiciously. "Are you kidding with me?"

"Not this time." Newt flashed a huge, reassuring grin and then looked at the sky. "It looks like we'd better get ready for the show."

"What show?"

"You'll see!"

Bree used the tent as a dressing room, and he changed in the open. He had the cooking clothes stowed safely in the bear bag, which was now suspended in a tree some distance from the tent. He handed Bree her jacket and a navy-blue beanie and stretched a black one over his head as he shrugged his jacket over his powerful shoulders. "You are going to get cold so put on the hat."

Newt pulled both sleeping bags about ten feet away from the tent. Then, he sat down on top of his sleeping bag and extended his strong hand to Bree, helping her sit down lightly on her own down-filled sleeping couch. After a little while, the cold set in.

"You're right. It sure is getting chilly," she said as she snuggled into her coat and zipped it all the way up.

"When the sun goes down out here, temperatures drop fast, even in the summer months."

"This isn't anything like Dallas. Usually, it stays hot all day and all night. I don't know how people lived there before A/C was invented. On summer days, I went to the gym to work out because the humidity was so unsafe."

"Sounds like Hell on earth."

"Now that I have this to compare it to, you aren't far off."

"So, you're starting to like it out here? I'd love to hear you say 'yes'." Newt reached for her hand and covered it with both of his.

They were so large, so warm, so comforting. "Yes." Bree struggled to keep her voice steady since she felt like she was going to squeak out her answer like a scared mouse. The way he looked at her with such affection was unsettling. She was off balance but knew he would catch her if she fell.

He pulled her in close and tenderly used two fingers to lift her chin, so he could look deeply into her dark brown eyes. She was the most beautiful creature he'd ever seen. Newt kissed her gently, respectfully, and then pulled back so he could see her expression. "Is that okay?"

"Yes," Bree answered breathlessly.

He kissed her again and she draped her long arms around

his neck and shyly kissed him back. Newt, aroused by her willingness, struggled to control his desire. She was certainly getting a rise of him, but it was too soon for them to take things any farther. They needed to know more about each other. The last thing he wanted to do was harm her.

Breathless with the kiss, they broke away and sat regarding the other with admiration infused with passion.

"I want you." Bree was panting, her eyes smoldering.

"And I want you, too, my sweet, but it's not time yet. We need to make sure my pet doesn't get hurt, and not taking time to build a good base for our relationship could mess things up. I'll tell you when we are ready."

Bree's sigh was edged with frustration, she pressed her head closer into his shoulder and let it rest there. Newt looked down and smiled. He loved having her head resting on him. She was safe. She was with him. They were both happy and she was all his.

The day faded and the darkness took over as they remained seated next to each other. The sky was cloudless, the moon nearly full, and a myriad of pinpricks scattered throughout the inky heavens.

Newt extended his arm and pointed toward a constellation. "There's the great hunter, Orion. See the line of stars that make up his belt? There's his sword." He and Bree had both long since stretched out and snuggled down into their respective bedrolls.

"I don't think I have ever seen so many stars in my entire life." Bree lay on her back next to him. They both used their jackets as pillows and had their arms folded underneath and behind their necks.

"I'm sure you haven't. I imagine there's a lot of light pollution in Dallas."

"Light pollution? You mean like trash in the sky?"

"Kind of. The light from large settlements dilutes the darkness, and the stars and planets don't show up as vividly. Also, the altitude here is over 9,000 feet, so we're above some of the thickness in the atmosphere. If we were on top of one of the fourteeners, we'd see even more clearly."

"What's a fourteener?" Bree was intrigued.

"One of the 53 peaks in Colorado that are 14,000 feet above sea level or higher. We're nearest to Mount Evans."

"We aren't going to hike that high, are we? That sounds really hard."

"Not this time. In the future if my girl decides she wants to climb Mount Evans, we will. Committing to the ascent of a fourteener is like planning an involved and complicated vacation. It requires lots of dedication and hard work."

"I bet you've climbed them all." Bree's admiration was evident.

"Only two. Longs Peak and Mount Evans. I did it when I was younger and seeking glory. It didn't take me long to realize that my desire to be in the backcountry wasn't about dominating or conquering it. Now, I spend time out here because I want to know something well and readily respond in love when it needs me." Newt wanted to say "she" instead of "it."

Bree closed her eyes to ponder knowing something, someone as intimately as Newt had explained his relationship to the wild. She thought about how much she would like to know him like that and to have him know her so well. Bree settled into Newt's warm embrace. Her breathing became slow and deep as she listened to the wind making the pine trees whisper secrets and tales of goodness and fell into time with the breeze. Soon, Bree from Dallas was fast asleep.

Chapter 11

Newt woke before dawn to find Bree snuggled next to him. She was shivering and seemed to be trying to climb into his sleeping bag while she still slumbered, so he was glad he'd given her that hat. She'd literally be freezing without it. Looking around, he realized they both had drifted off in the open and underneath the stars. The fire was completely burned out and cold.

Newt climbed out of his sleeping bag, leaned down, and carefully scooped Bree into his powerful arms, sleeping bag and all. He carried her and gently set her inside the tent and pulled the emergency blanket from his pack. Draping the silver cover across the sleeping Bree, Newt arranged his bedding outside the tent and settled into his still-warm bedding to watch his beautiful pet sleep. Her long lashes touched the tops of her high-boned cheeks and tendrils of her fawn-colored hair escaped the beanie, forming a halo around her face. Newt propped himself up on one elbow and rested in wonder of ever finding her. He'd deliberately built his life around his love of solitude. He'd wanted to be open and avail-able to observe the miracles in the natural world without distraction. Now, he sat watching unexpected miracle as she slept. She was no longer shivering and at last resting well. Newt sighed happily, let himself sink into his sleeping bag and joined her in the land of dreams.

Dim light filtered through the tent fabric as Bree's eyes fluttered open. Looking at the ceiling of the tent, she realized that Newt must have moved her. Bree smiled. There was a silver blanket draped over her sleeping bag showing he'd taken of her while she slept and made sure she was safe and warm. Bree quickly climbed out of her bedroll and pulled on her cooking clothes, which Newt set out for her before he left the campsite. She quickly dressed, laced up her hiking boots and pulled on her jacket. She was eager to find out what adventures he had in mind for her today.

Newt was at the fire ring where he'd cooked dinner the night before. Lively flames were dancing underneath the grate that rested on the edge of the fire.

Bree could see steam rising from the spout of the coffeepot she'd carried in her pack yesterday. The smell of coffee greeted her from several yards away. "Good morning," Bree chirped as she approached the fire, hoping she would be able to soak up some of the heat emanating from it.

"Good morning! I trust you slept well once I got you warmed up earlier this morning." Newt extended a metal camping cup full of fresh coffee to her. "Do you want me to put anything in it for you?"

"No, black is fine. Gosh, it smells amazing."

"Off-the-grid coffee is *the* best." Newt poured coffee into a canning jar with a piece of cloth secured over the top to capture the grounds and served as a filter. "I'm not a fan of cowboy coffee," he said as the dark liquid drained into the cup. "That stuff isn't filtered and there's nothing worse than chewing coffee!"

"Agreed. To the mountain barista!" Bree extended her cup and Newt tapped it with his.

"We are off to a beautiful start." Newt set the cooking pot full of water on the grate next to the coffeepot. Once the water boiled, he'd make a satisfying oatmeal with a no-grain granola knowing the fruit and nuts in the mix would provide energy for the day's excursion.

"This is really good coffee. Thanks." Bree blew over the top of the cup to cool it and then quietly sipped it as she let her eyes pan over the meadow and the lake in the distance.

"Thanks. I have another hike planned for us today. We'll catch dinner on the trail before we come back to camp." Newt dropped large scoops of oatmeal into the mess kit bowls.

"You aren't going to shoot an animal, are you?"

"Not today, but sometime soon. Remember, my pet, you need to eat whatever I provide for you." Placing the multitool with the spoon out into a bowl, he handed the hot meal over to her.

"Of course, I'll listen to what you say." Bree began digging in and once again was surprised at how she had suddenly become so hungry. "Why does everything taste so good out here?"

"I've wondered that myself. I think food is more delicious because I have to work for it. Whether it's foraging or hunting or packing it in with me, I am an active part of obtaining it and not simply standing in line and handing over some cash for it. I understand I work for cash, but it's abstract. Up here, the relationship between working and eating is so obvious. If I don't get off my ass, I don't eat."

"Things are less complicated up here, aren't they? In Dallas I used to feel so overwhelmed by decisions. I have a huge closet full of nice clothes, but most mornings I couldn't find anything to wear."

"I find the clear choices, the simplicity offered by the life up here refreshing. It frees up headspace to observe and be grateful for what's around me." He looked at her with a particularly appreciative smile.

Noticing his steady gaze, Bree felt a rosy blush creeping into her cheeks. She also felt a flutter of excitement in her belly and a thrill, almost electric, between her legs.

"Let's get camp tidied up and bear-proofed," Newt said, noticing her pleasant awkwardness. "We may get to see one today."

"One what?"

"A bear."

"You *want* to see a bear?"

"Under the right conditions, of course." He pointed to the shotgun and patted his sidearm as he flashed his powerfully assuring smile. "You'll see. Observing one isn't as common as you'd think. Like I said last night, bears are shy by nature, so seeing one is an amazing experience."

The sky was bright with wispy clouds streaking the distance. The scene looked just like a picture on a souvenir shop postcard. Bree couldn't believe how the colors were so vivid in the landscape, and she couldn't help but feel invigorated. Bree could never once recall having the outdoors infuse her with such joy and vitality. Her connection to Dallas was fading just like the washed-out colors in Texas, and it seemed her life there belonged to someone else.

Newt led the way across the expansive meadow. They walked around boggy spots and along soft dirt paths made by animals in the area. At one point, they skirted a beaver pond.

Newt pulled Bree back into the willow rushes so as not to spook the large, swimming rodent as it carried a branch pinned between its long incisors.

"It looks like a muskrat, only it's as large as a dog!" Bree felt breathless as she watched the beaver cut through the water and flap its tail on the surface before diving under the water.

"Unlike the swimming rodents you refer to, beavers are fascinating and industrious engineers as well as community members. Also, they have neater looking tails than muskrats."

"I have to agree. How do you know so much about them?"

"I get quiet. I observe. I listen."

"It's not easy to do in general, is it?"

"No. I had to learn how. You can too."

Bree couldn't help but beam at his confidence in her ability to learn new skills.

They stood up to leave the dam, and Bree held Newt's hand as they walked across the meadow. She fell in step behind him when they had to walk single file to climb an incredibly steep trail. The switchbacks were so sharp that Bree felt it would be better to climb across the trail and up to the next level. She attempted it once and ended up pitching forward and scraping her elbow. Newt turned to see her sprawled across the undisturbed area between the switchbacks. He retraced his steps and extended his hand to pull her up.

"Listen to me. There are trails for a reason, and you need to stay on those durable surfaces. More people than the two of us travel these trails and not staying on them creates erosion." His expression was stern and serious.

"It would be easier to just climb up," she said tersely.

"Easier isn't the point. Enjoying the space and preserving it for someone else to appreciate is the reason there is an etiquette code out here. You know I will not tolerate your being disrespectful to the wild spaces."

"But it's so hard!"

"And it will pay off. Trust me." Newt turned back to the incline and began planting his feet as he ascended the trail. Bree fell in behind him, still grumbling despite her panting from exertion. Newt was acutely aware of her annoyance. He considered that he might have to get stricter with her when they return to camp. However, once the climb to the ridgetop was finished, Newt's resolve to discipline her flagged. He watched her beautiful eyes grow wide with wonder and fascination as the panorama of a new valley lay before her.

"My gosh! It's amazing!" Bree struggled to say the words since she was still panting from the climb. She looked around and was overwhelmed by feelings of humility and awe.

Newt stepped up beside her and turned her to look at him. Placing his fingers below her chin, he lifted her face to him and kissed her deeply. She returned it without hesitation. Their lips parted briefly, and she pressed into him for another. His hunger for her swelled and threatened to overtake him like snow in an avalanche. *Skies! I want her with me. She's such a courageous little thing, and I want more than anything to have her, to care for her!*

The surface of the ridgetop was nothing more than a gravel swath approximately five feet wide. With nowhere to comfortably sit, Newt took Bree's hand and lead her ten feet down from the top on the opposite side. He found a rock outcropping where they could both rest and kiss until they were breathless. Newt pulled her close to him, so they sat hip to hip while they contemplated nature's display before them. Neither spoke. There was nothing words could add to the discovery of the place and each other.

After a while, Newt helped Bree stand up, and she felt her feet touching the earth. He took her hand and led the way back to the top of the ridge and over to a small group of trees set back and away from the steep trail. Finding a cool, shady spot near the roots of the pines, Newt sat down and began foraging in his pack. Bree sat beside him and looked at him expectantly.

"I'll tell you about our next adventure while we eat our lunch," he said as he tore a large hunk of sourdough bread from a homemade loaf and handed it to her with a thick slice of cheese.

Bree waited until he began eating before she attacked her portion. Once she tasted the food, she realized she was ravenous once again. She watched Newt thoughtfully tear off a bitesize hunk of bread, slowly place it in his mouth, and chew it with deliberation. He was so handsome, and Bree knew, as she watched him, that the hunger she had wasn't just for food. She felt a deep yearning for him in her core. Pulling her water bottle from her day pack, Bree took several deep gulps to help the dry bread move down her gullet and cool her longing.

"I think we will go back to the lake after this so I can catch our dinner. One of the streams leaving the lake fills the beaver pond we saw earlier. I usually have good luck catching a trout or two in that area." Newt popped piece of cheese into his mouth. "Good, huh?"

"Good," Bree agreed. "Do I have to fish too?" Bree began to wrinkle her nose in disgust before she realized she was challenging him. She immediately looked contrite.

"Not this time, pet." Newt noticed the change in her demeanor when she started to get stubborn with him. Indeed, she was learning.

"Great." Bree tried not to sound too relieved.

"Just like everything out here, a person could spend a lifetime learning how to think like a fish. Many do just that. Flyfishing is a huge recreational draw for the area. I don't enjoy catching fish that way and would be bored stiff if I had to commit to just one outdoor activity. I think flyfishing for sport is like golfing. Both bore me. I fish to eat."

Compared to the rigor of their climb up the ridge earlier that day, the descent back to the meadow was enjoyable once they separated from the wicked twists of the trail from the mountain's top. Bree merrily followed Newt through the boulder field surrounding the lake.

"It's hard to believe these rocks we are walking around and crawling over were thrown here with the help of water, isn't it?" Newt asked as they were clearing the big rocks and approaching the soft path along the shore of the lake.

"Water? How do you know?"

"Look up at the top of the glacier ice. Do you see how the rocks spread out along the edges of it and at the base? It's called an alluvial fan. The natural phenomenon occurs in lots of areas, most commonly at the mouth of rivers with sediment, but here in the mountains, they are sometimes comprised of boulders like this one. If you think about the water cutting these canyons, the idea of it moving a bunch of rocks isn't at all farfetched." Newt began skirting the lake, and Bree walked beside him. He was delighted when she timidly reached out for his hand and he folded her hand in his.

"I never realized there was so much to learn about the world. I never stopped to think about it until you started showing me these things."

"What did you used to think about?"

"Well, when I was in Dallas, I used to think about meeting people and wanting them to like me. I thought a lot about how I wished my body looked different or what kind of image I wanted to create with my clothes. Dallas is a huge place, but I see, now that I'm away from it, the world I lived in seems small. The more I learned about life and how things worked while I lived in Texas, the less I liked it. I always spent a tremendous amount of time struggling to find the right 'look' if you know what I mean."

"I don't." It was Newt's turn to look repulsed.

"It all seems so far away now. Strangely, my life before is starting to seem so trite."

"Maybe it is."

"Funny, but the day you rescued me was the day I decided I wanted something different for myself."

"What did you decide you wanted?"

"At first I thought I wanted what all of the girls I knew desired, to be a princess and have her demands met immediately. I thought I needed to be admired by everyone and have others wish they could be as amazing as I was. I wanted to be more than great, I wanted to be stellar, even perfect. The day I hiked away from the resort, I didn't know what I needed, or what I wanted, or even what I was searching for, but now I think it was adventure. When I got hurt on the trail, I decided I wanted safety." She turned to regard Newt. "Is it possible to find both?"

"Why not ponder that for a bit and let me know."

Chapter 12

B ree followed Newt as they approached the stream and wandered down the trail a little while before they broke off through the willow rushes. He stopped at a solid outcropping from the bank where a naturally smooth dip made the rushing water easily accessible.

"This is usually a lucky spot, so I'll see what I can catch. Here," he said as he handed her a thin book and continued, "There are lots of flowers in the meadow this time of year. Go on ahead and take a gander with this field guide. See if you can identify them, but make sure you stay close by."

Her eyes lit up. She was surprised by his confidence in her. "Of course," Bree said brightly.

"Good girl." Newt smiled at her enthusiasm, set down the shotgun and started unpacking his fishing gear.

Bree moved back through the rushes and took special note of a rock that looked like a turtle. She made a point to remember it as a marker for finding her way back to Newt and followed the game trail. She scanned the meadow for color and wasn't disappointed. Golds, pinks, and various purples peeked out from the lush green grasses. The striking reds of the Indian Paintbrush and the sunny faces of the sunflower-like Gold flowers filled Bree with wonder. Many of the flowers had blossoms growing in globes, some near the ground, but others sat atop long stems. The faint purple Sky Pilots with fern-like leaves and balls of small flowers grew in among the golden Alpine Avens and looked like yellow moss roses. Bree moved to one group of blossoms that stood tall. The Snowball Saxifrage display was breathtaking in its variety of colors, yellow, pink, and white flower balls standing high above frilled paddle leaves shaped like those of pansies. No suburb in Dallas could boast of a more beautifully inspired garden than what she was experiencing right now.

Bree, enthralled with the flowers, was moving further from the stream where Newt was fishing. She found herself at the edge of the pond where she and Newt had seen the beaver earlier that morning. Hoping to get a clear look at the animal's tail should it swim near to her, Bree quietly walked near the dam, knelt, and waited, but the beaver never showed itself. Bree finally gave up and began to walk toward the rushes on the other side of the dam. She was watching where she was placing her feet since the ground was uneven and possibly slippery in the muddy places when she heard a great snuffle. Bree stopped in her tracks. Whatever made that noise sounded big.

Slowly, she looked up in the direction where the sound emitted. Approximately thirty yards from her was a male black bear standing on its back legs just like a giant man. The bear was nearly seven feet tall, but it looked the size of a European dragon to Bree.

She held her breath and soon she began to gulp the air as

she tried to prime her lungs to shriek. She struggled to capture her breath, but it continued to escape her, as if someone had just punched her in the gut. It seemed forever before her lungs finally filled up and she could muster a scream. And scream, she did. The high pitched, spine-chilling shriek carried. The bear heard it, dropped to all fours and immediately began popping its jaw and stomping its feet. Tears streamed down her face as fear washed over her in sickening waves. Her voice alternated between sobs and shrieks. The bear, unsure of what it was being confronted by, continued popping its jaw and stomping. *Snap, thump, stomp. Snap, thump, stomp.*

Newt was packing up his gear after landing two beautiful rainbow trout when he heard the alarm. Dropping his fishing gear and grabbing his Henry shotgun, he sprinted in the direction of the cries. He eased his pace as he heard the sounds outside of Bree's screams. It had to be a bear. He knew the animal might charge if it felt cornered, and Bree's panicked articulations had to be scaring it. Carefully, Newt peered around the willow rushes which served as a blind and were hiding him. Yes, it was a bear all right. A huge male. The poor animal looked as if he were having to deliver a speech and would rather be anywhere other than where it was standing. The animal had no idea what was confronting it. Newt put the shotgun in his sling and quickly closed the gap between himself and the panicking Bree. He stood behind her, grabbed her across the chest with one arm and covered her mouth with the other. He held her tightly until she quit struggling.

"Listen to me," he said in a low growl. "That bear feels cornered, and we are going to move away slowly and quietly so he can go his own way. Do you understand me? No more noise."

Bree nodded, and Newt removed his hand. "Now, slowly walk backward. Do not, I repeat, do not take your eyes off him, or try to run. If you run, he will have you within a few strides. Understand?"

Bree again nodded as Newt helped her step back. The bear quit the jaw popping and watched as the distance between it and the possible threat increased. The stomping ceased when Newt carefully maneuvered himself and Bree around the willow rushes and disappeared from the bear's sight. Carefully and quietly, Newt parted the branches in time for them to see the bear hurriedly trotting off in the opposite direction.

Once assured of the animal's escape, Newt turned to Bree's wide-eyed, tear-streaked face. "What the hell! Why were you scaring that poor bear? Don't you know he could have hurt you and probably would have had I not showed up in time. You cut off his escape, otherwise, he would have avoided you completely!"

"*I* scared the bear?" Bree sobbed, once again gulping for air. "What do you think it did to me? Can't you see I'm absolutely terrified?"

Newt looked stricken. He circled his arms around her and pulled her in close. "Of course, you're scared. I'm sorry I yelled at you. You're safe. I have you now."

Bree melted into him. Her knees were shaking, and her body trembled with waves of adrenaline-induced sobs. "I'm sorry. I'm sorry."

"Hush now, there's nothing to be sorry for," he murmured as he gathered her even closer to him. He held her until her sobs quieted. Kissing the top of her head he continued, "You scared me, and I can't imagine what I would have done had you been hurt. I would have never, ever forgiven myself." He took Bree's hand and led her back to his abandoned fishing gear and walked over to the stream to retrieve the fish on the stringer. Holding them high, he smiled and said, "We're lucky the bear went in the opposite direction because he just might have helped himself to our supper."

Bree smiled too, comforted by his presence. As they walked in an easy and comfortable silence across the meadow and back to the campsite.

Once they were back in camp, Newt gutted the trout and buried the viscera away from the cooking area. Now that they had encountered a bear, he was glad he'd taken the extra precautions to keep them safe. He doubted the bear they'd encountered earlier was food conditioned, so it was unlikely to visit their camp and ask for a handout. Newt got the fire started for cooking. He and Bree changed into cooking clothes and started preparing to cook. She came to join him as he was getting freshly filtered water to boil. Newt was pleased to have her close by so he could protect her. He knew Bree was not looking forward to eating those lovely trout he'd bagged, so he was determined to make them as delicious as he could.

"I have a surprise for you," Newt said as he poured steaming water into the camping cups. He stirred the mixture and handed a cup to Bree as he began blending his own. Bree looked down to see hot chocolate with mini marshmallows floating along the edges of the chocolate.

"Thanks!" She was delighted. "I especially like the kind with the little marshmallows." She smiled. "I have fond memories of Christmas days in Texas. Myra, our cook, used to make chocolate like this for everyone."

"Nice! You go ahead and just sit back. Enjoy your chocolate while I get our supper together. I need to let the fire get a bit hotter before I can set the fish packs in to bake." He reached over to grab another dry branch and added it to the flames. "That means we get to enjoy another cup if you're game."

"Yes, please," she said after finishing the first cup and

holding it out to Newt. "After seeing a live bear close up, I'm pretty sure I need a double."

He grinned as he refilled her cup with more chocolate before he handed it back to her and did the same for himself. He took a sip and set the cup aside before he spread out pieces of tinfoil and lay the fish on top of them. He stuffed dried jalapenos and pats of butter into the bodies, added instant brown rice and some dried mushrooms and then some water. He folded the foil into a packet around the fish and placed each pouch into the coals of the fire ring.

"It won't be long now." He sat back on his haunches and gave Bree his winning smile. "Unlike our hobo stroganoff the other night, fish cooks fast. You might learn to like it because you get to eat sooner when it's on the menu."

Bree wanted to deny that she could possibly enjoy eating something that she'd seen swimming freely in the lake, but she also had to admit that with only five minutes under the coals, that trout was beginning to smell darn good.

Newt, too, could scent the cooking fish and his stomach rumbled in anticipation.

"You're hungry," she observed. "It's starting to smell really good."

"Perhaps my pet will be a bit more open-minded when she tries my gastronomic creation. It's nearly finished." He moved the foil packages out of the coals with a small green branch from a pine and pulled it to the rock surrounding the fire. Using a wooden spoon and spatula, he quickly extracted the small bundles from the heat. Steam filled the air in front of him as he unfolded the foil envelopes and dumped them onto the mess-kit plates. Grabbing one of the multi-tools and laying it on the side of the plate, he handed the steaming portion to her.

"Thanks," Bree said, taking the plate from him and trying to hide her surprise. The fish smelled so good.

"Let me give you a trout-eating demo." Newt gently pulled at a corner of the gray, black and white spotted skin which came free from the pink flesh. "Eat the pink part slowly. There are lots of bones in these little guys, so you are going to have to pick your way through. I will show you how to take out the spine and most of the ribs, but you still need to be careful."

Bree tried to hide a cringe. She was so hungry, and the food smelled so good. She decided she had to give taking the bones out of the fish a try.

Newt lay his trout on its back, used his multi-tool knife to dislocate the trout's back bone and pulled. The spinal column and most of the rib bones yanked free. "Simple as that," he said with a grin. "Now, your turn."

Bree mimicked his demonstration and the bones of the fish released cleanly from her portion.

"Nice job! And now we eat." Newt lifted the flaky flesh into his mouth.

Bree took a tentative bite and was surprised at how delicious the creature she'd seen swimming in the lake tasted. "This is amazing!"

"When it's this fresh, it really doesn't need much seasoning at all."

"It's so good! I swear I never knew fish could taste so amazing."

"I'm sure there are fish in Dallas."

"Yes, catfish. It's disgusting and tastes muddy. Just roll up a wet newspaper and cook that because I am sure it would taste a ton better."

"Well, I'm glad to introduce you to something better," Newt said with a smile.

The sun long ago moved behind the ridge, and the darkness crept toward the fire and surrounded the two people in communion with it. Neither Bree nor Newt spoke as they sat together closely on the fallen tree trunk, pleased with their own thoughts and each other's company. Bree was content with the quiet and now had no urge to fill the stillness with words. She enjoyed the silence and sat with Newt listening to nature fill the world with sound. Her life was changing. She looked sidelong at Newt, noticing his dark, thick hair and how his beard looked well-kept despite being in the wilderness for two days. She'd known him only a few days, yet he seemed to know her better than she knew herself. Bree had something she wanted to say to him, but she was hesitant to break the spell. The encounter with the bear demonstrated his devotion to her, and she wanted Newt to know how much it mattered. She finally spoke up, "Thank you for introducing me to all of this." Bree swept her arm in front of her body to wave at the dark, wild place before them.

Newt turned to face her and then pulled her close to him. "And thank you for showing me all of this, Bree from Dallas." Newt touched her nose with a pointer finger. You are showing me unknown territory too."

Bree blushed and looked away.

Newt continued, "You know, I'm not fond of people. I like my own company and don't mind going for days without uttering a word to another soul. But Bree from Dallas, I have become quite fond of you. I didn't want to like you because I thought having someone else in my life would only keep me from accomplishing my plans for my life. You aren't detracting from it one little bit. You are enhancing it."

"May I ask you to do something for me?" She felt hesitant. She hoped her request wouldn't seem ridiculous to him.

"Of course, my sweet."

"Because of this beautiful relationship, I am changing.

Dallas feels like a lifetime ago. Maybe I was just another person when I lived there. Now, I feel like I am becoming someone else. Either way, my memories of Texas are fading, and I'm not sorry because I feel that I'm finally finding out who I really am and where I truly belong. Would you please call me Bree and not 'Bree from Dallas' anymore?"

"Gladly and pleased to meet you Bree–just Bree," Newt said with promise. She smiled and lay her head on his shoulder. He touched her chin, and she tilted her head toward him. Taking her lips with his, he kissed her deep and long. Neither felt they could get close enough to the other. Newt pulled her onto his lap where she sat astride him. They engaged in another long, deep, and passionate kiss. Newt struggled to not roughen up her mouth with his beard and his wanting lips.

Bree could feel him rock hard beneath her, and she deliberately moved her hips back and forth over his length. Newt placed his strong hands over her sweet butt cheeks and pulled her in closer, pressing himself into her center. She gasped with the increased pressure, and he hungrily took her lips with his. Holding her buttocks with one hand, he unfastened her cargo pants with the other. Newt fished his hands inside the gap between her flesh and the cloth and caressed her silky skin. Bree gave a seductive moan as she circled her arm over his broad and powerful shoulders.

"Before this goes any further, I need to know if this is what you want?" Newt's eyes were smoldering. "I also need you to know something else. I love you."

Bree instantaneously became wet with wanting, knowing full well that she was the object of his desire. "I love you, too. And yes, I want you." She gave him a level gaze as he pulled her t-shirt up and over her head and let it fall behind her. He released her bra and tossed it aside as well. Then, he hungrily took one of her nipples into his mouth. Letting his tongue dance around it until she gasped with pleasure.

His teeth grazed the edges of the turgid tip and Bree yelped in surprise. The sensation was incredible. Bree held on tighter and arched her back, giving him free rein of her naked torso. She was delighted to hear him offer a low growl of delight. He kissed her other nipple while his strong hand covered and massaged her other breast. Newt began kissing her mouth deeply, hungrily. Their desire intensified, and Newt pulled her off his lap and set her feet on the ground. Letting both hands slide over her curvaceous hips, he unfastened and pushed her cargo pants down to her boot tops. Newt knelt and worked the laces free on her boots before pulling them and her pants from her feet. He plucked away her wool socks and stuffed them inside her boots, and Bree stood before him naked except for her lacy panties. He removed his own boots and socks and placed them alongside hers. Newt stood up and pulled his t-shirt over his head, exposing his broad shoulders, muscular arms and chest.

Bree watched him with appreciation and increasing arousal as she stood before him in the moonlight. She was the object of his desire, and everything felt right. She looked at him with her eyes rounded with longing.

Newt reached out and placed his palm between her legs where his hand remained still. He wanted her to get used to his hand, he gave Bree a wicked grin as she stood still and waited for what he would offer next.

When he remained still, she whimpered, "Please," and bit her lower lip.

"Please what?"

"Please keep touching me." She began to sway slightly and let her head fall back as she leaned into his hand, which became more unyielding as he turned it to its side and let his thumb play against her lacy crotch. Again, she continued to rock back and forth over his hand and was struggling to not give in to the tension he was creating for her. Each stroke she initiated made her wetter with wanting him.

"Go on. You don't need to wait for me now, since I'll be with you soon enough." He pulled her panties down as his husky voice gave her permission to fall into her passion. He stroked her wetness, and Bree immediately felt pulsing in her core, causing her to moan with overwhelming sensations. She nearly crumpled when he pressed a finger inside her. Newt caught her and pulled her closer to him, as he continued to play in her velvety folds, smiling as she squirmed and whimpered until her climax began to fade.

Standing up, he freed himself from his trousers. He pulled her toward him, as he sat down again. Bree climbed onto his lap, once again astride him. He pressed himself against her body and felt he would explode when she pulled herself closer to him. Newt moved her leg up to his hip and then placed the other leg on the other side. Bree hooked her ankles behind his back, opening herself to him. Pressing the tip of his member into her, he delighted in her primeval moan. He needed no more invitation and carefully moved his entire length into her.

Bree wanted to scream with the yearning he was building in her. Newt didn't move at first and held her still as he filled her with his rod of desire.

"Oh, please! Please!" she cried as she squirmed and moved herself over his length, slowly at first. She moved faster and with increasing urgency.

Newt help her glide her velvety softness along his shaft, moving himself into her and away. Finally, the tension became so great they let themselves be completely swept away. Newt still inside her, held her tightly as they clung to each other waiting for their blissful shudders to subside. They continued to hold each other until Bree stepped off his lap and stretched her beautiful limbs. Newt took her cue and pressed his strong arms into the sky.

She sat down next to him while they put their boots on. They gathered their cooking clothes and walked naked to their tent. They pulled their sleeping clothes from the bear bag and replaced them with the cooking outfits. Both knew their sleeping clothes would remain in a pile beside them in the tent, just as they both knew they would sleep beside each other naked and as lovers.

Chapter 13

Newt woke before the sunrise, the pre-dawn chill prickling his skin into goosebumps. He and Bree were cocooned within the large pocket of both sleeping bags he'd zipped together. The edges of the sack lay draped to the side because they'd slept close together, spooning the entire night. Newt basked in having her pleasing form snuggled next to him. He pulled her closer, enveloping her body, determined to protect her from anything and everything. Breathing in the fragrance of her hair, which smelled of fresh air and wood smoke, Newt couldn't imagine she ever paraded around wearing heavy fragrances or abundant styling products. She told him about the other Bree, but he struggled now to recall the woman he'd first met. She was becoming a child of nature as well as an adorable charge, and Newt looked forward to the days they would spend together. He'd known her for such a short time, and yet he had become comfortable with her and couldn't imagine ever being with anyone else. Newt thanked providence, closed his eyes, and let himself be lulled to sleep by the light morning breeze and the song of the Vespers sparrow.

The morning light shined past the tent flaps and brightly moved over Newt's face. He was still holding Bree tightly and nuzzled her neck affectionately as he made little growling noises to wake her.

"That tickles," she said and giggled sleepily, then hunched her shoulder to try and keep his prickly beard away from her sensitive neck which wasn't successful.

"I'd like to provide you with more than a mere tickle." He pressed his growing arousal into her as he brushed his hands over her belly, her rear, her breasts. He continued to snuggle into the curve of her neck.

"I'm listening." She smiled, her sleepiness turning to mist and fading away. She felt the warmth of his touch, and it kindled her desire for him.

Newt continued to caress her and marveled at how responsive she was to him. Her body was a new and beautiful territory, a frontier waiting to be revealed and opened to him. He wanted to survey it all, including her heart, her mind, and her soul. They, too, promised him the adventure of discovery. She was soft in all the right places and having her curvaceous rear pressed against him was intoxicating. He pressed his hands against her shoulders and neck, massaging them as his arousal grew with each caress. He could hear her faint pants and pressed his cheek to hers before he traced the outside of her ear with his tongue and ran his hand down her back and over her sweet butt cheeks. Newt pushed his hand over her hip and placed it between her legs where he found her wet. She wanted him.

Bree yelped with delight. He had her body so awakened she felt she would fall over the edge in no time. He was following the lines of her ear with his tongue, and Bree moaned deeply as she arched her back, pressing her backside into him. She flinched in surprise at first but then in wanting when he slipped his hand over her pelvis and pressed his hand firmly between her legs. She knew he could feel her yearning for him. He pressed his pulsing member against her. She rolled over to face him. "Let me see you."

Newt pulled her close and playfully touched the end of her nose with his finger. "You have to ask permission, my sweet, and not tell me what to do. I know what is best for you, so let me decide what you need."

"Please, Sir, may I look at you?"

"Of course, my darling." Newt released her and enjoyed her appreciative expression when she saw all of him. Bending down, he captured her lips, kissing her deeply and pressed her legs open. He moved his hand between them and pressed it against her firmly. Newt gazed upon her beautiful face and deep brown eyes that beamed with admiration and desire for him. "You are such a lovely pet," he said. She dropped her gaze demurely and then reached up to pull him closer. "Now tell me what you want from me."

"Oh, please, Sir." The anticipation of him entering her was becoming unbearable. His turgid member lay between them. She could feel it hot and throbbing and wanted nothing more than to have him inside her.

"Please what?" he asked with a wicked grin, teasing her.

"You inside me. Please, may I have you inside me?"

Newt gave no answer before he granted her wish. Instead, he gently and deliberately pressed himself into her velvet folds and her pleasurable tightness. He struggled to put aside his excitement and wanted to be certain she was completely satisfied. He moved within her and instantaneously felt her muscles pulsing around him before he gave himself over to the wonder of her. Her panting become heavier until she whimpered sweet cries in her climax, and he, too, was swept away by the power of her experience. They met in their shared ecstasy.

Their passion subsided but they refused to move apart and lay together connected physically, spiritually, and emotionally, basking in the afterglow of desire and the warmth of the new day's sunshine.

Chapter 14

Whal and Niven found the place they were searching for. While there was no sign of the occupants, a quick examination of the cabin's interior indicated the residents' absence was temporary. Fresh food chilled in the refrigerator and windows weren't boarded up. The men also discovered a new backpack in the single bedroom and uncovered Breanna Phillips' wallet, which contained her driver's license and credit card. Her phone's battery was completely depleted, but the men knew it didn't matter. There was no service in the area.

Whal sat under a distant tree, taking occasional glances at the homestead through a pair of high-power binoculars. He and Niven had staked the place out for two days and saw nothing, but Whal had an intuition that was about to change. He sent Niven to the small mountain town near the store so Niven could call the boss. The area near the Mercantile was the only place they could get cellphone reception. Mr. Phillips would let the men know what he wanted done next.

Both Newt and Bree wished to stay in the wilderness for one more day of adventure followed by another night of discovering each other.

"I want to stay another day," Bree said wistfully. She looked down and pouted.

"I need to return to get that order done. Taxes and supplies don't pay for themselves," Newt answered as he looked at the panoramic view, enjoying the clear morning.

"I guess." She stuck her lower lip out further.

"You've never had to be concerned about money, have you?"

"No. My parents always made sure I never wanted for anything, after my mother died and my father immersed himself in his resort empire, he gave me a generous stipend until I finished college and found a good job. It was hush money to keep me from complaining as well to keep me hobbled and beholden to him. I'm grateful that's all changed."

"What's changed?"

"Being pinned under my father's thumb."

"How so?"

"Before I came back to you, I found out my mother left me an inheritance my father knew nothing about. I don't have to go back to Dallas—not now—not ever."

"But you said you are 'the face' of his company. Don't you think he expects you to come back?"

"If he does, he will have to come get me. I seriously doubt he'll be able to track me. I didn't tell anyone other than the store owner and Owen where I went." Bree let her gaze slowly sweep over the meadow, the distant lake, and the ice of the glacier that fed it. "Beautiful," she whispered.

Newt leaned over to kiss her cheek. "My sweet, you are adorable. You are lovely. You are refreshing. You are my special girl."

Bree's eyes shone with excitement. "It took a noble man like you to see it, and I am so grateful for you."

It was Newt's turn to stutter and fidget with embarrassment from her high praise. She was the most beautiful creature he had ever laid eyes on, and he knew he would do anything to keep her safe and happy.

———

Their sleeping clothes were now another trail outfit, rumpled, but also cleaner than their fragrant cooking clothes. Newt showed her how to break camp, and once their sleeping place was cleared, they moved down to the cooking area to erase their presence there as well.

Newt set about making his famous off-the-grid coffee, only on the cookstove this time. He didn't want to leave the remains of a fire on the day they left and felt at ease knowing the firepit was cold when he left it. The water began boiling in the coffeepot, and Newt began to pour it over the t-shirt filter. Once the liquid was strained, he removed the filters and handed Bree a cup.

"I can't believe how good coffee smells up here. I was never a coffee drinker until I met you." She looked coyly over her cup.

"I've worked a long time to perfect my craft, and I enjoy having an appreciative audience," he praised her, smiling back. "This morning, we have a surprise for breakfast. Something that's almost as sweet as you are." Newt handed her a bowl with golden granola and fresh berries. After pouring canned milk over the grains, he sat back, grinned and watched her light up.

"Raspberries? Miniature strawberries? I didn't know they grew up here!"

"Lots of things grow up here." Newt sat down on the tree

limb beside her. "You can forage with me today if you're interested."

"I'd love that," Bree said brightly. She looked forward to learning how she could contribute and how she could help him.

Newt balanced his bowl on his knee and reached his arm around Bree to pull her close to him. They had been in the wilderness only two days, and the bond they forged was natural and surprisingly strong.

After breakfast, they shouldered their packs and started hiking the trail that led up the side of the ridge, out of the rambling meadow and back to the beaver's pond.

Newt stopped to set his pack down and surveyed the pond. "We'll cut a few cattails while we are here. They taste a little bit like cucumbers."

Bree offloaded her pack as well. "That sounds lovely. We haven't had too many fresh things since I came to see you."

"You're in for a treat." Newt began pressing the water plant tendrils aside. "This is the best time of year to gather them. They look like hotdog buns and not tails of cats." Newt reached his hand out to her and pulled her closer to the bank where they looked over the water. "Do you see any of those buns out there?"

Bree scanned the tops of the plants and noticed some inside the forest of green fronds. "There! I found one over there!"

"Good girl!" Newt said as he looked around, following her gaze. "We'll bring them in, and I have just the tool for the job." Newt pulled the jackalope knife from a sheath fitted onto his belt. "A very special girl gave this to me, and I am looking forward to getting to use it for the first time."

"Oh, you like it!" Bree squealed her delight.

"Of course, I like it. You gave it to me." Newt reached down to the base of the plants she'd identified. The blade on the knife wasn't intended to do this kind of work, but he wanted her to see him use it, so she knew her thoughtfulness mattered to him.

He sawed the long stalks and turned around to show her a large handful. Bree gathered them into her arms and watched as he freed another bunch. She held the fronds and watched while he cut the long stalks down for travel. They poured filtered water over the tender shoots, and folded them into a clean cooking towel, before snuggling them just under the flap on the top of his frame pack.

Bree was elated to be included in the foraging, and it sparked her curiosity about the world around her. She followed Newt on the well-defined trail and barraged him with questions.

"What kind of bird is that?" she asked as one flushed from some brush and ran across the path ten feet in front of them.

"It's a white-tailed ptarmigan."

"Why is it running? Shouldn't it be flying?"

"It's related to a forest grouse, and they prefer to run if they can. If it must, the bird can fly."

"What does a ptarmigan eat?"

"They eat leaves, flowers, bugs, and berries this time of year. In the winter they live on conifer needles as well as buds and twigs from the alpine willows and alders."

"What's a conifer?"

"It's a word for trees that have needle-like leaves and bear cones, like the pine trees around us. So many questions!" He stopped on the trail, reached over to touch her arm and brought her to a halt. He turned her to face him. "What's gotten into you?"

"I woke up to find the world is wondrous. I want to know more about it because I want to know more about you."

"I'm happy to tell you anything I know." Newt pulled her off the trail and held her tight, resting his chin on top of her head after giving it a gentle kiss.

The trek back to Newt's home seemed to Bree to move faster than it had when she had first followed him into the wild. She wasn't looking forward to their return to his home or he to his work. She wanted to go on more adventures. While they retraced their previous route, Bree felt like she was seeing much of it for the first time. Now, she stood on the rock outcropping where Newt had brought her only two days before and consciously planted her feet on the earth and felt connected to something grander than her own experiences.

Newt was a planner and took calculated risks, and while they stopped for lunch, Newt pondered how he was a creature of habit. He had spent a lot of time in the Mount Goliath Natural Area and had discovered places where he liked to eat, liked to sleep, and liked to rest. He returned to these places frequently. He realized that while he'd been preaching to Bree about discovering new things, he hadn't exactly been practicing it himself. Bree was leading him into new territory. He never anticipated she would show him something he didn't know much about—a close, intimate relationship.

They were sitting on a rock cluster eating trail mix, venison jerky, cheese, and crackers while they gulped large drinks of water. A couple of camp robber birds jumped down from the bush where they perched to size up the couple. Newt and Bree sat quietly. Newt was waiting to see what the birds were planning. One was bolder than the other and took a couple of hops toward them. It turned its head sideways as if it were trying to see what chance it had for a smash and grab. Not seeing an opportunity, the bird took a few more hops closer.

"Does it want to steal our lunch?" Bree asked quietly.

"You bet it does. They are unscrupulous raiders."

Newt was munching on a cheese-topped cracker, which he set on the end of the log before reaching past Bree to grab the plastic bag of trail mix, which was sitting on top of her pack. In a split second, the bolder jay took to the air, pelted toward them and grabbed the cracker and cheese with its talons before it flew away cawing in victory.

"It stole your lunch!" Bree's eyes were wide with disbelief.

"It took the bait I set out for it. I saw how it was watching you and the trail mix. Maybe it had you pegged as an easy mark. A cracker and a bit of cheese was a small sacrifice. We got to keep the trail mix." Newt was grinning widely as he set it on the rock.

"I've never had a bird get that close to me."

"Those guys are bold, but with time, you'll become good at reading them and possibly outguessing them." Newt reached over and turned her face to his. "That is, if you want to see them often enough to discover how they behave." He kissed her deeply and found her hungrily kissing back. He pulled her in close to him. While she was distracted, the second bird swooped in and snatched the trail mix with its feet. Neither Newt, nor Bree cared since they both knew the trail mix was the very last thing they were hungry for.

Chapter 15

Newt's uneasiness refused to be ignored and he was on edge as he and Bree were following the trail to his homestead. They were just about to emerge from the forest when he noticed boot prints on the trail. They weren't familiar to him. It wasn't unusual for hikers to be passing through on his property, since Newt had no problem with folks using his property to get somewhere else. These tracks, however, were clearly present both on the trail and off numerous times, and it appeared someone was conducting a search, but for what? As far as Newt knew, the release date for the poachers was a few months off, and Newt figured it would still take the men a few months to track him if they were still interested in a confrontation. Newt's intuition told him this discovery somehow concerned Bree. He stopped on the trail and grabbed Bree's arm as she trudged past him.

"I need you to stay behind me while we walk the rest of the way," Newt cautioned her as he unlatched the holster for his sidearm.

"What's going on?" Bree tried not to sound alarmed.

"I'm not sure. Call it a gut instinct. Just do what I say."

Newt pulled the .44 Mag Ruger from his holster and held it ready. They emerged from the trees, and his suspicions were confirmed. A black Dodge Ram dually sat in the forest shadows, and two men with holstered sidearms and Kevlar vests were approaching them.

Newt stopped on the trail, pushing Bree behind him. "Hey guys, this is private property. Unless you have business with me, you need to move on."

Whal and Niven stopped several yards ahead of the couple. Bree kept trying to peer around Newt's form, but his strong arms held her safely behind him.

"We're looking for a hero," Whal said.

Newt wasn't impressed. "A hero you say?"

"Indeed, I'm Greg Whal and this is Ted Niven. We're security for the Mount Goliath Resort and need to find the woman you rescued. She's the owner's daughter, and he is quite concerned for her safety. Do you happen to know where she is?" Whal and Niven both tried to peer around Newt's form.

Newt held Bree close behind him, "If you want to talk to them, I'll see no harm comes to you," he said under his breath.

"I guess it can't hurt to send reassurance to my father that I'm okay."

Newt stepped aside.

Bree recognized the men from the resort. She'd never had occasion to speak to them, but she knew they had represented themselves correctly. "Hello." Bree warily regarded Whal and Niven. "Thank you for going to all the trouble to find me and deliver my father's message. Please tell him I am doing well and will notify him when and if I decide to return to Dallas."

"Begging your pardon, Miss Phillips," Whal began. "Your father insists you come home. He is returning to Dallas within the week and needs you back at the estate."

Newt stepped in front of Bree a second time. "The lady said to give her father her best regards. You both need to leave my property. Now." Newt slipped the sling for the Henry rifle from his shoulder.

Niven, palms up in front of his chest, stepped in front of Whal. "You don't have to get forceful. Our employer asked us to deliver the message. We've done it and now are on our way. Aren't we?" Niven said as he turned to look straight at Whal.

"We are," Whal said, his voice seething with hostility and frustration. Both men reluctantly walked back to the truck, climbed in and drove away, spewing gravel and mud behind them as the pickup's wheels grabbed traction.

Bree again peered around Newt's strong body as they both watched the dually drive away.

"That won't be the end of it," she said. "My father is used to having his way about everything."

"He won't about this if you want to stay with me. Tell me what you want, and I will see that you have it. Don't worry, pet. I'll keep you safe."

Bree now stood in front of him and pressed her head into his chest. She was shaking uncontrollably. He wrapped his strong arms around her, enveloping her in the safety only he could provide, and held her until she calmed. "Come on, let's go inside and get a drink of water, and I'll make us some tea." He took her hand and led her like a frightened child to the comfort of his kitchen. Newt could see Bree was feeling better after they walked to the cabin.

They dropped their gear by the back door. Newt fished out the fresh cattails they'd harvested earlier that morning and placed them on the kitchen counter before he poured two glasses of water. Bree sat down at the table as he brought the drinks to the table and then sat down to join her.

"Don't worry, pet. Nothing that you don't want is going to happen."

"I'll bet my father shows up here."

"And I will send him away just like I did the security guards."

Bree gave him a half-hearted smile and nodded.

After they had a cup of catmint tea, Newt decided to diffuse the tension created by the unexpected encounter with the security guards, and suggested they unpack their gear and get it ready for storage. The task was complex, and he knew it would keep Bree's mind occupied.

Bree was surprised to learn Newt was so particular about treating equipment correctly for the next trip. Trying to remember everything he was telling her and keeping the details straight was a welcome distraction for her. "Why is there so much to all of this?" she asked.

"It's just easier to put things right at the end of the trip to reduce prep time when I decide to go out again. I want to pick up and go whenever I feel like it and enjoy the freedom of grabbing my pack, throwing in a few clothes and some food, and hiking away to relax. I don't want to get stressed out with details before I leave."

"Interesting. I never had to plan like that. If I forgot something, I'd just buy a replacement when I got to my destination," Bree offered.

"How do you feel about that now?"

"I think it's wasteful."

"I think you're right. Look at you, becoming so sensible." Newt flashed his indulging smile. "Since you have been such a good pet, I have a treat for you."

"What is it?"

"An outdoor shower. Washing up will take your mind off the earlier drama and help you relax."

"Outside? You have a shower outside?"

"I set it up for the summer, and guess what? You get to go first. Come on." Newt stood up and stepped outside. He began walking toward the lean-to where he worked on his furniture.

Bree jumped up to follow him across the yard area. She saw a small paddock created from split logs fastened to the side of the lean-to created a privacy fence. A wooden gate blocked a clear view of the enclosure. Newt opened it, so Bree could see past him. Flat gray stones formed a rudimentary floor, and a shepherd's crook was fastened to the fence at the far end of the enclosure. A heavy, black, fabric-covered plastic bag filled with approximately five gallons of water was hanging from the hook, and dangling from the bottom of the bag was a nozzle. A plastic milk crate was set on end to support a tan, grainy bar of soap, which sat on top of a chipped blue saucer.

"See? A shower!" Newt looked pleased with himself.

"Doesn't it get cold out here?"

"It can. That's why I set this up for the summer months. For the milder fall and spring days, I bring out the bag of water after I've warmed it up inside. That water in the bag right now has had all day to warm up, so you get to go first. Isn't that great?"

"But won't it still be cold?"

"Remember, my sweet, I keep telling you this isn't what you are used to. It's another adventure. No matter what the water's temperature is, I can assure you that after being in the woods for two days, you are going to appreciate how good it feels to rinse off the dust and the smoke and the sweat. So, are you ready?"

"I suppose," Bree said hesitantly.

"Great. I'll go get you a towel. Go ahead and get started. I'll be right back."

Bree stood in the shower stall as she watched him leave, sighed, and began to disrobe. She had serious doubts about this.

Bree was naked and standing under the showerhead and looked up at the bag. She just knew there was no way the water was warm and was already getting cold from standing on the rocks in the fresh air. She figured she'd better get started before she got so chilled, she wouldn't be able to get warmed up. Bree grabbed the nozzle, pressed the lever, and gasped audibly when the water hit her exposed skin. She underestimated how warm the water would be until it raced over her body, and just as Newt promised, she relaxed as it washed away the dust and the smoke and the exertion of their trip.

Bree had her back to the water source and was rinsing the oatmeal soap from her long, tawny hair when Newt opened the gate to give her the towel. She looked toward the noise, finding him standing before her, transfixed. She smiled and continued rinsing her hair and then her body in the luxury of fresh running water. Newt waited with a large, multicolored, striped beach towel draped over his arm while she finished washing up and began wringing the water from her hair as she walked over to him.

"Stay right there." He moved toward her with the towel spread out with both his hands. "I am going to dry you off, my sweet pet."

Bree did as she was told and stood in the chill of the air as he pushed the towel over her locks, using his fingers to massage her scalp to pull the water from her tresses. He employed a corner of the towel to delicately dry her face, his dark eyes intently holding hers. Taking one end of the terry cloth length, he dried her neck and then her shoulders. He bent down and took each of her nipples in his mouth after he passed over her breasts with the towel. The thrill of his kisses made her shiver, yet she stood still for him. Newt dried her belly and kneeling before her, he carefully rubbed the towel down one leg to the top of her foot. Moving to her other foot, he rubbed back up her other leg and playfully nuzzled the tawny mound between them. A deep moan escaped her, and Newt flashed her a wicked smile. He stood up and walked behind her as he began drying the backs of her legs, stopping to caress her rear end and playfully pinching each butt cheek before he dried her lower back and moved up to her shoulder blades. He pushed the towel over her collarbone. The ridgeline of her neck muscles was tense, so he began to work the tightness out of them with his strong fingers.

Bree felt as if she no longer had bones when he finished massaging her and nearly fell into his arms. Of course, he caught her when she began to crumple.

"Did my sweet pet like that?" Newt looked deeply into her large, brown eyes.

"Yes."

"Yes. What do you want to call me now?"

"Yes, Sir."

Newt then wrapped the towel around her, swept her up into his arms and carried her back to his cabin and into his bedroom where he set her down on the bed.

"Now, I want you to stay right here until I get back, or else." He waved his pointer finger at her. "You know what happens to naughty girls."

"Yes, Sir." Bree smiled brightly.

Newt wasted no time washing up. While wrapped in another beach towel, this one with circles in primary colors on it, he used the reflection in the cabin's front window glass to comb his hair and beard before he went inside. He saw Bree sitting on the bed, exactly as he left her.

"Let me comb your hair," he said as he sat down next to her and took the wet locks in his hands. He gently moved the comb through the strands, working up from the bottom and was careful not to drag the comb through her tangles. Newt enjoyed pampering her and once the snarls were all gone, he gently draped the front strands behind her ears. "Beautiful," he said as he looked at her appreciatively and kissed her forehead.

Bree's hair was now neatly combed, and her loins were on fire. Newt looked upon her with such approval after he'd finished taking out her tangles. She fully expected him to make an amorous advance. Instead, he reached for fresh clothes and got dressed, Bree didn't even try to hide her disappointment.

"Don't pout," he warned her. "The daylight is nearly gone, and we need to finish getting our equipment put away and our dinner prepared. Get dressed. Then come out to the kitchen to help me."

Bree stubbornly looked down at her hands, said nothing and did not move. Newt made note of her poor attitude and left the room. Once he was gone, she reached for her pack and pulled out a pair of yoga pants and a lilac long-sleeve top. Stuffing her feet into a pair of black plastic flats, she shuffled out to the kitchen and flounced down onto a kitchen chair. She certainly wasn't going to do as he said.

Newt gave her a stern look and sat down in the other kitchen chair. "Come here, pet," He said, his words were resolute.

"Why?" Bree's eyes grew wide.

"Why? Because I asked you to. Why? Because you are being childish and want to get your way. Throwing a fit is exactly how you do not get what you want from me."

"But I—"

"Now." Newt patted his leg. "Come here and stretch yourself over my lap."

Casting her gaze down, Bree trudged over to him and lay across his powerful legs.

Newt reached around her waist and pulled her pants down, revealing a lavender pair of lacy panties which he also pulled down from her lovely rear. "You can expect to be spanked when you act like this."

Immediately, Bree felt a swat that was so swift and stinging it left her breathless. Three more followed on the heels of the first. She whimpered as three more smacks landed upon her upper thigh. It stung even more than her butt cheeks which were now beginning to burn. Bree struggled as she tried to keep herself from squirming away. While she wanted to avoid the heat spreading across her backside, Bree realized that she had disappointed him and began to cry. The last thing she wanted to do was to let him down! Her body went limp as she sobbed. "I'm sorry. I'm sorry I didn't listen to you, Sir."

Upon hearing her weeping and apology, Newt immediately stayed his stern hand and turned it instead to comforting her. Carefully and kindly, he massaged her reddened skin. He struggled to contain his arousal as his hands moved over the beautiful slope of her rear. "You are such a good girl. I want you to listen to me because I'm making sure you are well cared for."

"I know." She was hiccupping now.

Newt pulled her up from his lap to stand before him and turned her so she could perch on his lap. He rocked her and stroked her hair until she began to breathe easily. Then, he helped her stand up. "Come on. We need to get our supper ready." Newt pull up her panties and yoga pants. He kissed her and circled his arm around her, steering her to the kitchen.

Dinner was canned chicken and noodle soup alongside cheese sandwiches and the fresh cattails. Bree was surprised the pond fronds really did taste like cucumbers. She helped Newt clean up and put away the dishes after they finished eating. Both were feeling the exertions and anxieties of the long day and were ready to turn in when the last dish was set on the shelf.

"Thank you for helping me, my pet," Newt said as he drew her close and kissed the bridge of her nose. "Do you know what the best part of this evening is?"

Bree shook her head.

"That I'm not sleeping in the front room tonight." He smiled.

Bree smiled too and let him take her hand and lead her to the warmth and security of his bed.

Chapter 16

The next morning, they tried to have a carefree day, but there was a constant and noticeable anxious undercurrent surrounding them. Both Newt and Bree wondered when the men would come back with another demand from her father.

Bree suspected her father was already enroute but didn't mention it to Newt. She trusted him to protect her since she knew her heart and wanted to stay with him. He would see to it that she remained by his side, never to return to Dallas unless she wanted to.

Newt was wrestling with uneasiness himself. He had no doubt that he could take care of himself with Mr. Phillips and his thugs, but there was a nagging doubt that his sweet Bree might be swayed to please her emotionally unavailable parent. Newt knew no matter what her decision, he would need to support her—even if it broke his heart

Bree was sitting on the front porch, watching. For what? Watching for trouble. Newt saw the lines of concern furrow her brow and decided to offer another diversion. His sidearm was strapped into his holster and he stepped through the front door of the cabin and grabbed the shotgun. He also took a canvas bag from a line of pegs on the wall and then stepped up to Bree.

"Let's get out of here and go hunting," he suggested.

"Hunting?" Bree squirmed, clearly uncomfortable with the idea.

"Mushrooms. Let's hunt mushrooms," he said in answer to her quizzical look. "And maybe find some greens for a salad."

"Salad! That sounds wonderful. I haven't had a salad since I got here."

"It won't be what you're used to. This will be a wilderness salad." Newt smiled reassuringly and took her hand before they headed toward the trees.

"Even better, I'm sure." Bree followed him as she threw the bag over her shoulder.

"Porcini mushrooms are probably the most easily identifiable mushroom in the area, and they don't have a toxic look alike in these parts. There's a spot on my property where they grow. It's a good time for harvesting since that torrential rain on the day I found you will bring us happy hunting. Stay close and pay attention. We are out for fun, but we both know we might need to deal with something unexpected.

Newt easily walked over the forest floor, and Bree kept pace with him until he stopped before a deep grove of aspen trees. She recognized the place. It was the forest area where Newt had rescued her. It seemed so long ago that she imagined that faeries, pixies, elves and gnomes probably lived in the place. Newt was standing still, looking down at the tree roots before he bent down to lift some matted, fallen leaves. He pressed them back into place. He stood up and faced her, his expression became serious, and his voice was stern.

"Mushroom hunters are secretive. We guard our harvesting spots, and I do not share my locations with *anyone*." His eyebrows furrowed and his face looked hard, but suddenly, his demeanor changed. She watched a large grin crawl across his face like a giant caterpillar and then he stretched his arms wide, inviting Bree to come closer. She did and he folded her into a hug and gave her a big squeeze. "Except for you, my sweet. I am delighted to share my secret place with you."

"So, where are they?" Bree couldn't help but smile at being included in his secret society of mushroom hunters.

Newt pulled the tangled leaves back to reveal the tops of what looked like red hamburger buns. The stalks beneath were thick and shaped like teardrops with erratic tan striping on the creamy trunks. The large brown caps resembled a wide-brimmed sunhat.

"They look like little people with big hats, don't they?" Bree asked.

"They do. I wouldn't recommend thinking about them like that. It'll make it difficult to eat them. *Rawwwr!*" He made a little lunge with his hands curled into imaginary claws.

"Eeek!" Bree feigned terror and then gave him a big hug.

Newt pointed out areas that held promise for a Porcini harvest. "Any mushroom hunter will tell you that if you find one, you need to stand still and look around. The odds are high that you will find more within twenty feet."

Bree did as he instructed but didn't see any places that looked promising. She gave Newt a dejected glance.

"Don't fret. Mushrooms are experts at camouflage. You'll develop an eye for them. Once you know what to look for, you'll see where they are hiding." He looked over the forest floor along the aspen trunks and saw a spot that looked promising and went to check it out. Bree looked over his shoulder when he bent down to reveal another group of red tops as he pulled back more damp leaves.

"They are good at hiding, aren't they? And they can appear overnight and remain maddeningly elusive." He smiled as he plucked them from the ground and handed them to her.

Bree grinned as she stuffed them into their foraging bag before skipping behind him to find their next escapade. Both hoped the day would remain quiet and calm.

The mushrooms were bountiful, and as they walked back to the cabin, Newt stopped to dig up a patch of yellow-headed dandelions.

"Why are you digging up weeds?" Bree asked.

"You think dandelions are weeds?" he asked curiously.

"They aren't? What are we going to do with them?"

"Remember that salad I promised you?"

"Yes."

"These are the greens," he said, holding the plants up by the roots.

"Uhm, sure." Bree was doubtful.

There was no one waiting for them when they returned to the cabin. Bree sat down on the porch to remove her boots and then went inside.

Newt heard her enter the kitchen, and looked up to see her smiling at him as he was at the small stand-alone counter preparing their foraging salad. He showed her how to cut the buttons from the large mushrooms while Newt chopped up the stems and mixed them with chopped water chestnuts and shredded cheese and stuffed the buttons with a heaping spoonful of the mixture. He wrapped the mushrooms in foil and headed for the door to go set them on the top rack of his propane grill. "Don't forget to add the flowers to the salad bowl and save those roots," he called over his shoulder.

"Why?" she shouted back. Once again, Bree wondered if he wasn't joking with her.

"The flowers are delicious, and I use the roots to make dandelion wine." Newt looked on approvingly as she worked.

The mid-day meal was wonderful. Since they harvested and prepared the food themselves, Bree thought everything tasted even better. After the meal, Newt made a mellow raspberry leaf tea and surprised Bree with squares of dark chocolate. "I've saved this for a special occasion," he said as he pulled the saucer from behind his back that held the broken chocolate bar.

Bree's eyes lit up. "Oooh, chocolate. How delightful. How decadent!"

The flavorful tea complemented the bittersweet chocolate perfectly, and they savored the dessert in quiet fellowship while they watched the world through the front window. Neither spoke of their fears as they waited for another confrontation with Bree's father or his hired men. When they saw the black dually truck drive into view, they were simultaneously alarmed and relieved. At least now the confrontation had come to them, and matters could be resolved.

Three men emerged from the truck once it came to a stop in the open yard. Whal and Niven both stepped from the front of the truck's cab before Niven moved to open the back door to the extended cab. A tall, refined, salt-and-pepper haired gentleman in a dark gray suit stepped from the compartment. Newt watched the man brush any wrinkles from his dress pants before the man purposefully strode toward the cabin.

"My father is here." Bree sounded defeated.

"Don't worry, pet. I'm here and protecting you." Newt stood up and took Bree's hand to lead her outside. They descended the stairs in front of the cabin and met the three men in the yard.

Whal put his hand out to stop the older gentleman from approaching the couple too quickly. "We don't want them to think we are aggressive, Sir," Whal told the man as Niven walked up and stationed himself on the other side of Mr. Phillips.

Mr. Phillips stopped his forward progress, but his voice carried with authority. "So, there you are, Breanna. I have been beside myself with worry."

Newt held Bree's hand firmly, helping her feel brave and confident. "What worry, Father? That you'd miss landing some important account without the 'face' of your empire?" Bree's voice dripped with contempt.

Mr. Phillips looked stunned and then pained. "Is that what you think, daughter? That the only reason I care about you is to promote myself?"

"Isn't it? Ever since Mom died, you couldn't have spent less time with me or cared any less for how I was doing. Your work always was, and still is your mistress. You never cared for us."

Mr. Phillips stood shocked and momentarily frozen in place. He carefully considered his words before he spoke. "You keep saying things like this, and I haven't taken the time to explain myself. It's my fault you've been so unhappy, Breanna, because I never took the time to discuss how much you matter to me. My darling child, I worked with complete focus out of dedication to you and your mother. Didn't I make sure neither of you wanted for anything?"

"That doesn't make up for spending time with us, Father. All we ever wanted was to have a relationship with you. When Mom died, you left me all alone unless you wanted me to do something! It wasn't fair, Father, and I am not coming home." Bree struggled to hold in tears while she straightened herself to stand as tall as she could. "I'm staying here with Newt. He loves me and cares about me and wants me to be next to him."

Mr. Phillips looked at the resolve his daughter was demonstrating. She was clearly determined. He took a glance at the powerful mountain man standing beside his daughter, and the father inside of him regarded the man with a blend of fear and of doubt. "Is what she says true?" Mr. Phillips asked, his voice filled with uncertainty. "She really thinks a nobody like you can care for her?"

"She knows her mind, and I am here to make sure her wishes are not only heard, but also honored." Newt's gaze was steady. He towered over Bree and looked formidable.

Mr. Phillips put his hands in his pockets before he spoke. This time his voice had softened. "Breanna, as you know I have rarely discussed my years growing up. You need to understand that I lived a meager existence. My father abandoned my mother and me to pursue his gambling, drink, and loose women. I took care of my mother, but I was only eight when he left. I didn't have any toys, Breanna. I had a cobalt medicine bottle I pretended was a car when I drove it around in the dirt—until someone stole it from me. I thought giving you everything you could ever want meant I loved you. Daughter, I am so sorry I didn't know what you needed."

"You didn't listen. I told you. And you forced me into being the posterchild for your stupid enterprises."

"Yes. Yes, you did, and you are right. I didn't listen because I thought I knew what was best. I, too, am lonely without your mother. I miss her very much, and now you are all grown up and are full of spirit and just like her. Daughter, I'm sorry I never told you why I had your likeness represent my ventures. I did it so I could always see you, even when I wasn't at home. Breanna, please understand I value your happiness over my holdings. Does being with this man make you happy?"

"It is. He is." Bree's jaw was set and her eyes, fiercely determined.

"Then stay with him, Daughter, and stay with my blessing."

Newt sighed, relieved that Bree was staying with him, and grateful Mr. Phillips could finally admit to Bree that he was misguided in his treatment of her. Bree's father unmistakably loved his child.

Bree released Newt's hand and ran to her father and threw her arms around the older man's neck, happy to hug the crying man.

Newt welcomed the three men to sit in the shade of the pines and enjoy a beer and pass pleasantries with each other. He was thrilled to see Bree joyfully talking to her father. Newt also noticed how broadly Mr. Phillips was smiling. Neither father nor daughter seemed reserved. Releasing the resentments and misunderstandings was freeing for both. Whal and Niven were pleased to kick back with a cold brew on company time. The air was festive when the three men walked toward the big truck to leave.

"I'll be waiting to hear of your nuptial plans, Daughter. Whatever you decide you need to make your ceremony special, will be my privilege to provide. Of course, I am reserving the right to give you away." Mr. Phillips smiled and leaned down to kiss Bree's cheek.

Bree embraced her father before he stepped up into the cab. Both had tears welling up into their eyes when Whal started the truck and Bree returned to Newt's side. Everyone waved as the truck eased onto the logging road.

Chapter 17

After her father left, they went back inside the house and sat down. They were both surprised and happy with the outcome of her father's visit. Newt eventually stood up and quietly left the room. When he returned, he held both rolled up sleeping bags they'd packed with them previously.

"Come on. Let's go outside," he told her and gave her a gentle smile.

Bree smiled and stood, following him outside.

They zipped their sleeping bags together again, and this time, there were fluffy pillows for them to rest their heads upon. Both lay stretched out on the earth watching the myriad of stars in the night sky above them.

The heavens weren't as clear as what she'd seen when she and Newt were in the wilderness. The display was awe inspiring though, and she was still amazed by the events of the day, but the greatest miracle was Bree had found the something more she was searching for. An owl was hooting nearby. She imagined that it, too, was voicing its wonder at the world around it. She and Newt lay together watching the stars until they both became drowsy and drifted to sleep

Streaks of morning light were just beginning to chase away the darkness when Bree awoke, shivering. She pressed her body closer to the sleeping Newt, and he pulled her in nearer as she placed the soles of her sock-covered feet next to his shins to warm up.

"Would you like to go inside now, or should I warm you up here?" he murmured in her ear, his beard tickling her cheek and neck. She could feel his hardness pressing into the small of her back.

"I imagine we'd get colder if we tried to make a break for it, and I don't think I can get any colder than I am right now."

"True enough," he said as he nipped her earlobe and began working his hands up and underneath her shirt. He brushed over her breasts, and Bree felt fire begin to spread through her. Newt pulled her toward him and then worked her shirt up and over her head. He set it aside as he licked her nipples and then playfully gave each one a love bite.

Bree held her breath as the pricks of pain turned to pleasure and the chill of the pre-dawn air washed over her. His hands roamed over her belly and then her hips as he pushed her yoga pants away from her shapely form. Once her clothes were bunched up at the bottom of the sleeping bag, Newt began removing his own Henley shirt and sweats. Bree wanted to touch him and convey some of the same admiration he was showering on her. She welcomed his touch, especially now that the greatest source of unhappiness in her life had resolved. She pressed her hands over his shoulders and chest. He felt so solid and so strong. She kneaded the tops of his shoulders and smiled. She heard him utter a quiet growl and he pulled her in closer.

Pressing his knee between her legs, he let his hardness rest between them as he bent down to kiss her deeply before releasing her lips, "Are you still feeling cold?" he playfully taunted.

"You've done an amazing job of warming me right up."

"Well, get ready, my sweet. Things are about to get flaming hot. Tell me, what can I do to keep building this fire?"

He began to move against her, and she felt like she would spontaneously combust. She was just starting to beg him to press himself inside her when he reached down between her legs and began to rub where the heat in her body had settled and centralized.

"How does that feel? Do you want more?" Newt pressed a finger inside her and began moving it with slow, deliberate strokes.

Bree was breathless and close to cresting the wave of desire that he was creating for her. "Oh, Sir, please be inside!"

Newt granted her wish, filling her hunger as he pushed into her. Bree cried out immediately and with every stroke, she whimpered louder, with a higher and higher pitch. She believed she could not possibly contain the bliss he was creating for her. Willingly, she let herself be taken by her climax and felt him top the pinnacle with her.

The fire in their bodies began to subside, and Bree looked up to Newt's eyes, which were intently studying her with shining admiration. "I trust you enjoyed our time together."

Bree smiled and pulled him close. Never could she imagine that she could feel like this, so wanted, so cherished, so loved.

In the morning, Bree begged Newt to make her new favorite dish for her breakfast. She wanted the oatmeal he made for them on the morning they left for the wilderness. There was no way he could deny her simple request. She grinned like a child who was given permission to eat chocolate cake for breakfast and promptly gave his neck a huge hug and kissed his cheek. They ate breakfast together when he promised her one more outing before he had to return to his furniture orders.

"Now that we know for certain that you are staying with me, how'd you like to try your hand at fishing?" he asked as he watched her attacking his breakfast creation with gusto.

"When?" she asked after swallowing a big bite.

"Today. I'll take you over to the pond where we saw the doe and fawn. There are usually a few trout hanging out in that deep pool."

"Are you sure I'm ready to catch a live fish?"

"I know you are. You stood up to your father and you told the whole world what you want for yourself. You just need to try something new."

Bree sat taller for his confidence in her abilities, and her smile brightened. "Then, yes. I am ready to catch a live fish today."

"That's my girl."

They walked along the trail that had taken them to the stream where Bree put her feet into the pool of icy mountain water for the first time. "I'm glad to see you so excited," Newt said.

"Do you think we will get to see another moose?" she said as she followed him up the trail.

"Perhaps another deer or maybe an elk, but you won't see a moose here. They like marshy areas and I've never seen one in my neighborhood." Newt stopped, turned toward her and reached out his arms to pull her close. "You know what the best part of any adventure is?"

Bree looked at him, her brow furrowed.

"Finding the unexpected. Just like I found you."

145

"I guess you are right. I never anticipated I would want to catch a fish, not that you are anything close to a fish." Bree looked at him, her eyes alight with her excitement.

"Exactly." Newt gave her a squeeze and they continued walking.

No wild animals made an appearance, but Newt showed Bree evidence of animals having been in the vicinity. Not too long before they had entered the area, a bobcat had marked a tree by scratching deep striations into the trunk and setting claw scrapes into the soft ground not too far from the tree. Newt also brought Bree's attention to the pungent odor of the urine markings.

Bree wrinkled her nose when he connected the odor to how the bobcat got it there.

They walked further into the area where the cat had claimed its territory, Newt noticed another animal sign. "This is probably what the cat was hunting for his dinner." Newt pointed at rabbit droppings near the underbrush. "You know, I, too, was looking for a rabbit when I found you. I don't think that bobcat will be as lucky as I've been," he boasted, flashing her his warmest and most dazzling smile.

Daylight was beginning to filter out of the sky when they finally arrived at the stream-fed pool, and Bree heard the insect songs. The whines of the mosquitos were the most noticeable. Newt made her stand before him as he sprayed her with a citronella mixture he formulated himself to repel bugs. They took their gear to the rock outcropping and began setting up their poles and prepared to drop baited hooks into the water.

Bree watched Newt open a plastic cream cheese container that had holes poked into the lid and a Christmas cookie tin that served as his tackle box. He set a net next to the other equipment.

"We're fishing with cream cheese?" Bree was hoping that was the case because she'd heard a lot about having to impale worms on the hooks whenever someone went fishing.

"Nope. I have maggots in there. Trout eat aquatic insect larvae among other things. A fat, tasty maggot is irresistible to a rainbow or brook trout." Newt was careful to gauge her expression as he talked up the maggots. She was clearly way out of her comfort zone, so he wanted to take care that she wasn't too uneasy or sour her on a relaxing hobby that also provided such a valuable food source.

"Don't worry, little one. I have three things I don't expect you to do on this first fishing expedition: put live bait on the hooks, remove the hooks from the fish, or put the fish on a stringer once we catch them. Your feeling squeamish will never do as far as I'm concerned, so I brought power nuggets for you to practice with." He continued assembling the poles and then put weights and bobbers on the lines.

"What are power nuggets?" Even after Newt provided an alternative, she still felt hesitant.

"They are like soft cat treats." Newt was delighted by her expression of clear relief as he handed her a burgundy red pole and black reel. Taking a power nugget, he showed her how to hide the hook with the delectable fish treat. He stepped up behind her, his chest resting against her back, as he offered pointers for her casting.

A few hours later, the sky was painted with an array of colors when they plunked their hooks into the water and in the fading light sat back together. Both watched the bobbers floating on the water's surface until some unsuspecting fish tugged and tried to swim away with a treat.

"Have you thought about what you want to do with regard to your old life after we return from this trip?" Newt pulled her close with his free arm. "While we have had a wonderful holiday, I need to complete my orders so I can bill them out."

Bree was quiet. She didn't know how to respond because she hadn't thought about *not* being with him.

"Look at me, pet." Newt lay his pole on the rock and put his leg over it lest it get pulled away from him. "I want you to know that your happiness and safety are my greatest concern. Tell me what you want us to do next Would you like to be married soon. I know I would."

"Yes, soon and in a simple outdoor ceremony."

"Consider it done! And after that? What would you like? Name it."

"I would love nothing more than to continue what you've started with me." Bree looped her arms around his neck, crawled into his lap, and kissed his cheek.

He pulled her close and kissed her lips deeply before he pulled away and looked into her lovely deep brown eyes. "How would you like to try your hand at carpentry? I'm willing to teach you. Are you willing to learn? Of course, you are going to have to work hard." He gave her a stern look before he gathered her close to him and kissed the top of her head, grateful that she chose him. "Indeed, you are nature's child and my sweetest pet."

Chapter 18

Several days after Mr. Phillips' appearance, Bree and Newt had set a date for their wedding. There were numerous chores to be done since they had been absent for several days, so once breakfast was over and the kitchen cleaned up, Newt promised to show Bree how to wash their clothes using rainwater; a large, anodized aluminum tub; soap shavings; and a plunger.

Bree had other ideas. She wanted to go for another adventure. "It's been forever since we've done anything fun," Bree complained. "Let's go do something fun, okay?"

Newt looked at her, his obsidian eyes stern. "Work first, *then* we play."

"But there's *always* work to do." Bree tried not to squeal as she was both begging and protesting.

"Yes. You are right about work always needing to be done. It's true that some people work all the time. I am not that person. You should know by now that I like to enjoy myself, too, but things have to get done. I don't have a staff to take care of chores."

Bree looked at him, her eyes pleading.

"My sweet girl, I have a list of things we must do before we go to the pond. Please understand that I have another reason for our going out later in the day."

"You do?"

"Yes. We may get to see more wildlife if we go when it cools off. You want to see more animals, don't you?"

"Yes."

"Then we go when I say so."

"Okay. May I help you with the chores?"

"I wouldn't want it any other way. We are together and living here, so you need to learn. Come on. We have clothes to wash. Newt reached out his hand and led her outside.

Bree looked around at the lean-to and the outdoor shower. She hadn't seen a washer in the cabin and was looking for it in the cattle shed.

"Washing clothes takes a lot of water, so if the weather is warm enough, especially in the summer, I try to wash everything and let it air dry. If you're wondering, I don't have a washer or dryer."

"I can't believe that. What do you do in the winter?"

"I do the same thing I'm doing now, only I perform the process indoors. As I was saying, I have a spin dryer to wring out the clothes and speed up the process. My clothesline is the fence for the outdoor shower. That's where I hang the clothes to dry. I use the shower door and other places around the cabin when it's cold outside."

"What's a spin dryer?" She watched as Newt ran water from the rain barrel spigot into the tub as he mixed in the soap chips with his hand.

"Oh, it's like a large salad spinner, only you use it for clothes. When I do my wash like this, I can't wash very many things at once. You can see why I have such a limited clothing selection. The trick up here is to layer. Often, I wear something for part of the day, so I don't have to wash it after every use."

"Gosh, back home I have so many clothes, I don't even know what I have. I used to stand in front of my closet in the morning thinking I didn't have a single thing to wear. All the while, the bars and shelves were brimming with things, sometimes with tags still on them."

"That sounds like a nightmare. I like keeping inventory slim. It makes it easier to make decisions and then act on them." Newt agitated the clothes with the plunger and swished them around in the soapy water with his hand. Then, he dumped the water over some tarps and other equipment from their trip and his work. "I'll get back to those in a minute. I try to use the gray water for washing other stuff."

"What's next?" Bree was fascinated by how he had such a seamless process and how painstakingly he worked to avoid wasting anything.

"I rinse these via the same method I just showed you minus the soap. It's your turn."

"My turn?" Bree was excited to be included in the work. It was new to her, and she wanted so much to please him. "What do I get to do?"

"You get to operate the spin dryer!" Newt pulled a clear plastic bucket that had a blue basket sitting inside it. There was a lid on top that had a pull-cord handle, much like one might find on a pull-start lawnmower. Newt sat down next to her, giving her a demonstration by pulling the handle and causing the basket to spin, forcing the excess water to flow out the bottom of a tube attached to the spinner.

"Now you try." Newt grinned widely and pushed the contraption toward her. Bree began to pull on the handle, and the basket inside the bucket began to spin. She was delighted. She pulled faster and faster, watching the basket spin furiously. The vibration from the movement, however made the spinner jump and then bounce away from her, spilling the clean clothes onto the ground. She sat, her eyes wide with horror and waited to see what Newt would say.

He admonished her saying, "You know, my pet, I have to do all of that work again now. And, of course, you know how strongly I feel about wasting water."

"Yes," Bree mumbled as she lowered her head and started fighting back tears as she waited to hear what punishment he would impose for her not being more careful.

Newt watched her. She was so lovely in her contrite state. Clearly, he should correct her for her carelessness. After all, he'd expressly told her he created the process to save water, and she should have been more mindful. But when he saw her sweet doe eyes begin to cloud with tears, he sat down next to her, pulled her close, and kissed the top of her head. "I know you didn't mean to spill the clean clothes on the ground. But you know I should discipline you for your carelessness." He looked directly at Bree. His voice was stern and unyielding.

Bree's eyes were wide with dread. "Yes, Sir." She looked down and began to shift uneasily from side to side.

"I also know you will be more careful next time. Let's not have any more bad behavior today." He pulled her to him, lifted her chin and looked into her brown eyes while he brushed a few stray tendrils of hair from her face. Newt smiled when he looked down at her and sweetly kissed her lips. "Our wedding day can't get here soon enough. You've stolen my heart of hearts, my sweet pet. I love you and I look forward to each day we have to spend together."

He held her close, wrapping her in his powerful arms, and Bree knew she had finally found that something more she'd been seeking. Here he was, the mountain man who loved and adored her, who completed her. A great adventure awaited them both, and Bree was eager to follow this new path with him.

Kitty Graham

Kitty Graham grew up at the foot of the Colorado Rocky Mountains where she soaked in the concepts of land management and resource conservation. She learned to appreciate the lessons of the mountains and the plains, the animals, and the history of the land. Her experiences with lengthy backpacking treks and subsistence farming impacts her writing and feeds her spirit of independence and self-reliance.

If she isn't reading or tending her garden, Kitty enjoys taking care of animals, mainly rescuing cats in need. What she appreciates most is spending time with her friends and family.

She currently lives in Northern Colorado where she can simply look outside her window for the inspiration she needs to bring her stories with happy endings to life. Kitty also writes as Sharon in the partnership writing of Sharon Ryan.

Kitty lives a quiet life with her husband of twenty-one years along with her three mischievous cats. She also has an aquatic turtle, which is her favorite animal.

Connect with Kitty Graham:
kitty.graham.author@gmail.com

Don't miss these exciting titles by Kitty Graham and Blushing Books!

The Mountain Man's Brat

Anthologies
<u>Daddy Dom Christmas</u>

Blushing Books

Blushing Books is the oldest eBook publisher on the web. We've been running websites that publish steamy romance and erotica since 1999, and we have been selling eBooks since 2003. We have free and promotional offerings that change weekly, so please do visit us at http://www.blushingbooks.com/free.

Blushing Books Newsletter

Please join the Blushing Books newsletter
to receive updates & special promotional offers.
You can also join by using your mobile phone:
Just text BLUSHING to 22828.

Every month, one new sign up via text messaging will receive
a $25.00 Amazon gift card, so sign up today!